The Thursday Night Club
and Other Stories
of Christmas Spirit

Steven Manchester

THE
ST●RY
PLANT

Studio Digital CT, LLC
P.O. Box 4331
Stamford, CT 06907
Copyright © 2017 by Steven Manchester
"The Thursday Night Club" copyright © 2014 by Steven Manchester
"A Christmas Wish" copyright © 2012 by Steven Manchester
"The Tin-Foil Manger" copyright © 2017 by Steven Manchester

Story Plant paperback ISBN-13 978-1-61188-280-3
Fiction Studio Books E-book ISBN-13 978-1-945839-14-6
Visit our website at www.TheStoryPlant.com

First Edition: November 2017

Contents

The Thursday Night Club

I

Jesse Cabral and three of his friends—Izzy, Ava and
Randy—gathered for their weekly *Thursday Night Club*
get-together on Izzy and Ava's front porch; they waited
for the group's final member, Kevin Robinson, to start
playing cards. They'd just settled in after their final college move and were ready to pick up where they'd left
off in May.

As college seniors, who'd escaped the dorms the pre-
vious year, Jesse and the small crew had quickly grown
to love the safe haven. A dim porch light illuminated
their late night games, assisted by a gaudy table lamp
that sat in their living room. On the interior sill, there
was an external speaker that could be accessed when
the window was open—which was most of the time.
Although the gang was good about keeping their music
at a respectable volume, the music was always on—as
they took turns running through each of their play
lists on their smartphones. An old, wooden table—its
green paint worn and chipped—sat near the porch rail-
ing and was surrounded by mismatched chairs. There
were several fixed items that sat on the table: an ashtray
for guests (none of them smoked, so it was almost like
a trap to unsuspecting guests who would face a serious

lecture if they ever lit up on the porch); a worn deck of cards they counted each time to ensure there were still fifty two; and empty peanut jars left by Jesse. Knotty pine floorboards led to a creaky glider that sat in the porch's corner; it was where Izzy and Ava sat—when they weren't playing cards—buried beneath Ava's grandmother's colorful crocheted afghans. An old steamer trunk, filled with pillows and throws, was used as a footrest or seat—whatever—while a framed photo of a black Labrador Retriever they called McGruff hung above the glider. As they couldn't keep any four-legged friends on the premises, it was the next best thing. The quaint space was an extension of the apartment's interior—just another room in a poorly decorated dwelling indicative of young people on tightly fixed budgets. Just beneath the porch, a recyclable bin was filled with empty wine bottles, pizza boxes and soup cans, while a plastic trash can overflowed with everything else. The rent—much like their college books—cost ten times its true value. But they didn't complain. Unlike most of the other college apartments in the area, this dump had a porch.

"I swear," Ava said, "it'll be nothing shy of a miracle if I make it through Professor McKee's class." Ava was a petite brunette with a cute face and shiny eyes.

Jesse grinned. "Well then, it's a good thing that miracles do happen," said the tall, lanky man.

"I'm serious, Jesse," Ava said. "She's inhuman." Ava shook her head. "She's honestly the coldest person I've ever had to deal with."

"Stop," Jesse said, shaking his short-cropped head, "she's not that bad. I had her for philosophy last year. I admit she can be tough, but trust me..." he grinned, "... under that hard shell, you'll find a warm, gooey center," he finished, his protruding Adam's apple nodding to each word.

"There's no way we're talking about the same Ice Queen," Izzy, the theatre arts major, chimed in. With long blonde hair and brown eyes, the laid back dreamer was actually speaking foul of someone—drawing surprised looks from the rest of them.

Just then, like a sudden Oklahoma twister, Kevin arrived on the front porch. Wearing the usual Irish skelly cap and secondhand clothes, he claimed his seat at the table. "Sorry I'm late, guys," he said, "but I broke down on the way over here."

"Oh no," Izzy said, concerned.

Kevin smirked. "My car's fine," he grinned. "It's just that a really sad song came on the radio and I had to pull over to the side of the road and have myself a good cry."

While Izzy and Ava slapped his arm, Jesse laughed. Randy shook his head. "You're such an idiot," he said.

Kevin's head snapped toward Randy. "Says the guy who ate a tuna fish sandwich made of cat food."

Everyone laughed but Randy—who sneered at each of them, while fighting back his own smile. "Yeah, real funny, clown," Randy said. "You mark my words, I'll get you back for that one too."

Kevin shook his head and looked over at Jesse. "I swear, ever since we dressed Randy in that Easter egg costume and hid him where no one would find him, he's gotten really mean."

Jesse shrugged and looked over at Randy. "Sorry, brother," he said, "I never realized we were supposed to look for you."

Changing the subject, Ava asked, "Why were you late, Kev?"

"It's probably that girl," Izzy added. "What's her name?"

"Marybeth."

"And she's the reason Kevin's cut back on the partying this year," Randy complained.

"Well, there are worse things," Jesse commented.

Ava nodded. "Why don't you bring Marybeth by to meet the group?" she asked Kevin.

He shook his head. "Because she'd never survive in this viper pit."

"What?" Izzy asked.

Kevin laughed. "We have way too much history together and almost everything we talk about is an inside joke."

"Gotcha," Ava said, and the others didn't question it any further either.

Jesse turned to Kevin. "Yeah, I have to admit it, Kev," he said, smirking, "you got Randy pretty good with that cat food sandwich."

"*Pretty* good? " Kevin repeated, nearly squealing.

Randy's eyes narrowed and his face turned red.

Jesse shrugged. "It wasn't bad."

"You're insane," Kevin said. "That gourmet sandwich is going down as legendary on this campus."

"You're the one who's insane!" Randy barked. "That prank was lame."

"And I suppose you could do better?" Kevin asked, defensively.

"Any one of us could top that stupid prank," Randy said, looking over at Jesse for back up.

Wearing a devilish grin, Jesse nodded in agreement.

Izzy and Ava looked at each other and shook their heads. "Here we go again," Ava said.

Excited with an idea, Kevin stood and held out his palm. "Okay. Okay. I know exactly how we can settle this."

There was quiet, each of them looking at the others and smiling.

"We'll make a bet," Kevin said. "Each one of us will kick in twenty-five cents. For a full week, we'll go out and have fun with any unsuspecting victim we can find. Exactly one week from tonight, we'll report back here and reveal our greatest prank. After an honest vote, we'll finally see who the true master is."

While the boys nodded their approvals, the girls surrendered in disgust.

"That's just asinine," Izzy said, "and you can count us out." She looked at Ava. "Aren't you happy we don't have testosterone?" she asked.

Ava nodded. "It's unbelievable. We're graduating from college in the spring and you guys are acting like you're still in high school."

"I know, right?" Izzy added "Real mature."

Jesse, Randy and Kevin sat at the table, grinning.

"Maturity has nothing to do with it, Izzy," Jesse said. "It'll be a wonderful exercise in male bonding. It's a guy thing, you know?"

The girls shook their heads again.

Kevin nodded. "That's right, though we all know who will dominate..."

"Yeah, me!" Randy barked.

"You're both wrong," Jesse said. "You boys just don't have the creativity to compete."

The three guys argued for a bit, each believing that he was the wittiest. Then, Jesse got back to the bet at hand. "I like the idea, Kevin," he said, "but there's one problem." He took a deep breath and grinned. "Randy

Steven Manchester

and I both know that you tell the truth like a used car salesman."

"Yeah, right," Kevin snapped but still took a moment to give it some thought. "Fine. We'll each record the craziness on our cell phones. The witness testimony of another player is the only other evidence that'll be allowed. Deal?"

While Randy and Jesse nodded in agreement, Kevin dumped one of Jesse's half-empty jars of peanuts onto the table and blew out the dusty remains. Grinning, he threw a single quarter into it. Randy and Jesse each added their quarters. Kevin screwed the cap back onto the jar and handed it to Ava. She shook her head and placed it into the corner of the porch.

"Any way to get disqualified?" Randy asked.

As Kevin began to shake his head, Jesse jumped in as the voice of reason. "Anything physically harmful or offensive should definitely be grounds for disqualification," he said, grabbing a handful of peanuts from the table.

Each man nodded his agreement, Kevin, a little more reluctantly.

"Awesome," Randy said. "Now we'll see who the real funny man is."

Kevin laughed. "And don't worry about the money, boys. This prank-master plans to give you both your quarters back. I'm just in it for the braggin' rights."

They each chuckled.

Kevin nodded and continued. "And that's braggin' rights for all time."

Jesse scooped another handful of peanuts into his mouth.

"Don't you ever eat anything besides peanuts?" Izzy asked.

12

"Yeah, peanut butter," Jesse said.

Ava laughed, which came out as its usual giggle.

Jesse stood and stretched. "Well, I have an early class tomorrow," he said with his mouth full, "so I'll see you good people around campus." He looked at Randy and grinned. "And beware, *everyone* is open game now." He chewed a few more times before swallowing whatever remained in his mouth.

Randy stood to join him. "I have to head out too," he said, turning his attention to Izzy and Ava. "See you all next Thursday night."

"Unless we see you first," Kevin blurted.

Randy shook his head. "You're so lame, Kev," he muttered.

Kevin stood and turned to the girls. "Ladies, we'll see you next Thursday."

Izzy and Ava nodded.

"Bye boys," Izzy said.

"And don't go getting kicked out of school for seventy-five cents," Ava added.

One final laugh echoed into the clear night.

2

Kevin and Jesse stepped into their first class of the day—Biology. Fifteen minutes into the mundane instruction, Kevin had an idea and grinned. On a clean sheet of white lined paper, he wrote a note: *Do you love me? Check Yes or No*, with a box beside each choice. He signed it, *Jesse*, and folded it in half.

Another ten minutes elapsed before the class was completely quiet and he decided to launch his attack. Without warning, he looked over at Jesse and yelled, "I'm not telling you again. Please leave me alone. I'm having a tough enough time in this class and I'm trying to pay attention."

While the professor's head snapped up, the rest of the class looked toward Kevin and Jesse.

Kevin shook his frustrated head, stood and approached the professor. He looked back at Jesse and smirked. "That guy who sits next to me just handed me this note," he said, pointing directly at Jesse, "and I think it may constitute sexual harassment."

The professor reluctantly grabbed the folded note.

"I came here to learn," Kevin added, dramatically, "not be treated like some piece of raw meat."

Still silent, the professor slowly unfolded the note and read it. Obviously trying to conceal his smile, he looked up at Jesse. "Please come see me after class, Mr. Cabral," the older teacher said.

"Thank you," Kevin said, returning to his seat.

"What did I do?" Jesse asked.

"Just see me after class," the professor repeated.

Seconds later, Kevin looked over at Jesse again and yelled, "I told you...the answer's no!"

When the class returned to the professor's lecture, Jesse shook his head and chuckled. "That's so bush league, Robinson," he whispered, "and it's going to take more than that to win a few quarters."

Kevin grinned. "Just so you know," he whispered back, "I would have checked yes."

"What does that mean?" Jesse asked.

Kevin nodded. "You'll see after class."

~ ~ ~

Across town, Randy stood at the counter of a fast-food restaurant, filling out a job application. He wrote the name *Kevin Robinson* on the first line. The young manager looked at him. Randy explained, "Whether it's fast food or telemarketing, I swear I'm going to get a job if it kills me."

The manager nodded compassionately.

~ ~ ~

Izzy and Ava were crossing the campus to head back to their apartment when they spotted a crowd congregating near the quad—the area cordoned off by yellow

15

crime scene tape. Curious, Ava headed straight for it with Izzy in tow.

The college campus was surrounded by groves of pine trees and a wood line filled with maples and oaks to the north, east and south. A pond and man-made waterfall bordered the east side of campus, with a heavy planked bridge designed for students to stand around and reflect on their existences. It was used more as a shortcut to the community center building where the campus bookstore, gym and cafeteria were housed. Cement pathways—that must have looked like one giant spider web from ten thousand feet above—wandered throughout the campus. Each path met at its center—its core—the campus quad.

The quad was a concrete octagon pit, with stairs that descended into a large cement pad at its center—several rows of benches sprouting out. Unless it was raining or snowing, students and faculty alike lined the quad stairs. It was a place where people studied, socialized, played acoustic guitar or even tried out old tired lines on the opposite sex. All roads led to the quad and though many folks could be seen spending time in their own world on their smartphones, it was still the main hub.

As Izzy and Ava reached the quad, they both began to laugh.

Dressed in all black, Jesse was standing in the middle of the concrete quad. His stoic face was painted white like a mime. A sign reading, CAUTION: MIME FIELD was propped up behind him.

"Oh, my God," Izzy muttered.

Ava shook her head. "What these stupid boys won't do to win a bet," she said.

The girls watched for a few minutes while Jesse mimed, atrociously. As they laughed, the large group that had gathered to watch was getting bigger by the second.

Izzy and Ava stepped closer to see a cameraman from the college's cable television show filming Jesse.

"It's being broadcast live across campus," Ava realized aloud.

"Give me a break," Izzy said under her breath.

One of the college's female reporters stuck her microphone in Jesse's face. "Sir, why are you out here today?" she asked.

Jesse said nothing but kept on miming—badly.

"To help save the environment?" she asked.

Jesse still said nothing.

"Is this some sort of protest?" she inquired further.

Jesse continued to mime.

"Perhaps you have a message to a society in ruins?" she suggested and looked back at the camera to flash her toothy smile.

Again, Jesse remained silent, offering his answer in dreadful mime.

The reporter turned to the camera again and smiled even wider. "Well, you heard it here first, folks. One brave soul has become a voice for those who don't have one..." She quickly glanced back at Jesse before nodding to the camera. "...without ever speaking a word."

Ava turned to Izzy. "Well, isn't that sweet?" she said, sarcastically.

"Absolutely precious," Izzy agreed. She thought for a moment and shook her head. "Doesn't it seem like a lot of work to make seventy-five cents?"

Ava nodded. "It seems like a lot of work to make seventy-five dollars," she replied and grabbed Izzy's hand to fight their way back through the crowd.

As they broke free of the mob, the girls looked back one last time. Jesse was still miming.

~ ~ ~

Between classes, Kevin's cell phone rang. He answered it. "Yellow?" He listened for a second. "No, I'm not interested in a future at Bob's Burger Barn," he snapped and listened again. "I don't care what the application says. Please don't call me again," he barked and hung up.

Kevin thought about it and grinned. "You're going to have to do better than that, Randy," he mumbled under his breath. "Much better." He laughed all the way to the sidewalk.

~ ~ ~

A few hours after the sun had gone down for the night, Randy was enjoying karaoke at his favorite local bar. He needed to sit through a few rounds of some very bad singing before his name was called. "Randy Duhon's up next," the DJ announced. Grinning, Randy stood and made his way to the small stage.

As the music started, he pushed play on his cell phone's voice recorder, grabbed the microphone and began dramatically playing to the crowd—singing the old tune, *Baby Come Back* from Player, completely off key.

The crowd ate up Randy's foolishness and started clapping. At the end of the song, Randy went to one knee and picked out the prettiest stranger in the crowd; she was with a group of female friends.

"That was for you, baby," he said. "Please come back. Drugs aren't the answer. The kids need you." He wiped his eyes. "I need you, baby."

"Ohhhhh," the crowd sighed, sympathetically.

In the middle of the applause, Randy placed the microphone back on the stand, and waved. "Thank you," he said. "I'll be here 'til Thursday. Please be sure to tip your waitresses on your way out."

As he exited the stage, Randy pushed stop on his mini tape recorder. He looked up to see the attractive stranger sneering at him. With a chuckle, he winked at her and left—the crowd patting him on the back all the way out.

~ ~ ~

The following day, Jesse stood out in front of the pharmacy collecting money for a fake charity. A flimsy cardboard sign reading, HELP STOP GINGIVITIS IN PERU was propped up behind him. He shook his empty cup at each customer that passed him by.

In the midst of some really bad looks directed at Jesse—a red-haired woman muttered, "Give me a break."

Jesse acted hurt. "Do you have any idea how bad everyone's breath is in Peru?" he asked.

"Bad enough to be stealing from people, I guess," she replied in a huff.

As she stomped into the pharmacy, Jesse laughed. Just then, another customer threw a dollar bill into his cup—oblivious to Jesse's sign or the phony cause it advertised.

Jesse looked into the cup and grinned. "We have enough for two packs of mints now."

Not five minutes had elapsed when Jesse stood in the middle of aisle four. He grabbed a box of anal itch ointment, lifted it high into the air and yelled toward the red-head, "Is this what you're looking for?"

Several other customers stifled their laughter before scurrying off to other aisles.

~ ~ ~

It was late afternoon at the Wonderland Costume Shop when Kevin paid the clerk for the rented gorilla suit.

"Little early for Halloween, isn't it?" the clerk said.

Kevin laughed. "No, not really." He reached for his wallet. "I think I'll pay cash for this, if that's okay?"

While the confused clerk cashed him out, Kevin smirked at his newest idea and left the store, lugging the heavy gorilla suit behind him.

~ ~ ~

The sun had just come up the following morning when Kevin was already hiding in the wood line near campus, dressed in the rented gorilla suit. *Time to give the world another glimpse of the missing link,* he thought. Every few minutes, he popped up and ran a few feet.

It didn't take long before two passing co-eds spotted him and screamed in terror. "I'm going to get the campus police," one of them yelled and took off running.

Her friend stood frozen, her mouth agape in horror. "It's...it's right there," she stuttered, "in...in the woods...over there." She put both hands to her mouth and screamed, "Oh, my God!"

Another female student rushed to the girl's aid. "Oh, my God, what is it?" she yelled, pointing at Kevin.

Oh crap, Kevin thought and turned to run away. *I've got to get out of here,* he thought, breathing heavily. *I could be disqualified for this.*

Just then, campus police sirens wailed in the distance, getting louder as each second passed.

Panicked, Kevin yanked off the stifling gorilla head and swallowed hard. By now, there were dozens of students moving toward the wood line in search of Sasquatch. *I've got to get out of here fast*, Kevin thought and ran for his life.

~ ~ ~

An hour later, Jesse was sitting on a bench at the local park, pretending to do some bird watching. He held a pair of binoculars an inch away from his face, while a can of black shoe polish stuck out of his back pocket. As a female jogger came past, he whistled. "Oh my Lord, she's beautiful," he said, excitedly.

Jesse could hear heavy breathing and looked up from the goggles to see the woman jogging in place right beside him. With a smile, he happily handed the binoculars over to her. "It's right there in the woods," he whispered, pointing.

The attractive woman immediately placed the binoculars to her eyes and scanned the woods. "I don't see anything," she whispered, pulling the binoculars away from her face and looking back at Jesse. There were two perfect black circles surrounding her eyes.

Jesse cleared his throat, as he struggled not to laugh. "I didn't see anything?" the woman said, panting.

Jesse smiled and took out his cell phone to discreetly snap a photo. "It was a baby raccoon," he said, taking the picture from his hip, "a little naïve, but really cute."

The jogger placed the binoculars back to her face and scanned one last time. "Nothing," she said and handed them back to Jesse—her eyes framed in shoe polish.

Jesse fought off the laughter and shrugged.

"Oh well," she said, mirroring his shrug, "thanks anyway." And she resumed her morning run.

Jesse waited a few moments before he allowed himself to laugh aloud. He checked his phone. The photo had captured the woman from her chin down. *That was dumb,* he thought, *I can't even get credit for this one.*

~ ~ ~

It was nearly dusk. Kevin was just closing his Psychology textbook on the stairs of the Campus Community Center when he heard the college's radio station report, "So the question remains, was there really a Big Foot sighting, or was it just some foolish kid who caused all the panic this morning?" There was a dramatic pause. "Campus Police are still investigating."

As a victorious smile worked its way into Kevin's face, his cell phone rang. He answered it. "Hello?" He listened and could feel his face burn red with anger. "I already told you people," he yelled, "I don't want to work at a dog shelter cleaning out kennels, so stop calling me!"

Kevin got up to leave. He was a few steps from the community center building when his cell phone rang again. He answered it and listened. "Now why in God's name would I ever want a career at Wally's Roast Beef?" he screeched.

~ ~ ~

That night, Kevin told Jesse, "It's so irritating. I get three or four phone calls every day from fast food joints asking when I can come in for an interview or from strange men wanting to meet me because my online profile seems *very interesting*."

Jesse laughed. "That sucks," he said, "but it could be worse."

"And how's that?" Kevin asked, disgustedly.

"Randy could have targeted me with all those mindless pranks," he teased.

Kevin was still shaking his head when Jesse blurted, "Oh, my God..."

Kevin looked up to find Randy's smug face looking straight at them from the television screen. Randy was sitting comfortably on the college's cable talk show couch. "Oh my God," Kevin repeated and slowly took a seat.

Brandt Swanson, the host, introduced Randy. "Today, we have Randy Duhon on the show. He's here to talk about some of the lonely folks in our college community who still find it hard to approach the opposite sex and ask for a date."

Randy smiled right into the camera.

In horror, Kevin and Jesse looked at each other. "Oh, no!" they said in sync.

"Thanks for coming on the show today," Brandt told Randy. "We appreciate it."

"Thanks so much for having me, Brandt. I'm grateful for the opportunity to speak to your audience today," Randy said, smirking into the camera. "I have some really good friends who are great guys, but they also happen to be incredibly shy. For years, I've watched them struggle to even speak to girls and I'd like to share their frustration with you today."

In horror, Kevin and Jesse looked at each other again. "Oh God, no!" they said in unison.

"When I first met Jesse Cabral and Kevin Robinson our freshman year, I thought they were both gay," Randy said. "But after a while, I realized that the feminine mannerisms and squeaky voices were just defensive mechanisms." He shrugged. "I guess they were just scared."

"I'm going to kill him," Jesse said through gritted teeth.

"Not if I get to him first," Kevin promised.

Randy looked back into the camera. "Girls, whenever you see Kevin or Jesse around campus, please be kind to them," he said. "They're both fighting to feel comfortable in their own skin." He shook his head and lowered his tone. "They're still trying to figure out who they are."

Kevin shook his head. "I hope Marybeth's not watching this."

3

The wet streets glistened beneath the streetlamps when Kevin and Marybeth pulled into the lot. Bent tubes of red and green neon hissed the word DINER; the exhausted R flickering like some cheap motel sign. A closer look revealed that the N was missing. DIER is what the billboard letters actually read.

They pulled into a row of cars parked right to the door and stepped out to face equal amounts of glass and polished aluminum formed in the shape of a giant bus. The restaurant looked like a trailer home right smack in the middle of a black-tar parking lot. *It looks like the perfect place to eat*, Kevin thought.

It was a tight squeeze past the candy vending machine where the new couple was greeted by another sign reading, *Please Seat Yourself*. They did. The booth was retro 50s, its bright green seat cushions cracked and taped. Kevin slid in right beside his smiling date. Marybeth was beautiful and sexy, with dark hair and eyes to match.

On the table, warm creamers, a sticky bottle of ketchup and an array of assorted jellies sat beneath a walled jukebox. Its selections were as outdated as the diner's elderly clientele. They dared not look under the table.

A gum-snapping waitress approached, coffees in hand. She smelled of home fries and scrambled eggs, saving Kevin and Marybeth the time of reading the *Specials* board. "What'll it be?" she asked with a smile.

"Two eggs over easy with bacon and toast," Marybeth ordered.

"An omelet," Kevin answered, "with everything in it."

The waitress winked and was on her way in a flash.

"I love eating breakfast food at dinner time," Marybeth said.

"Me too," Kevin said and grabbed her hand. For a moment, he scanned the place and allowed his mind to take in his surroundings.

Without breaking his frantic stride, the cook acknowledged the new order being put up. He was as thin as a scarecrow with a moustache to match. He was quick, his dual spatulas clanging melodically against the sizzling grill. A day's worth of sweat and food remnants stained his once white uniform, proof that he'd already worked his fair share. Still, he never slowed. After dropping some cubed potatoes into the deep fryer, he cracked four brown eggs. With the other hand, he reached for some cheese. Kevin sipped hot coffee and silently hoped it was his meal in the making. It was still too early to tell.

While some oldies tune played like white noise in the background, the place was awash in a chorus of friendly conversation. From the memorabilia that cluttered the walls, it was like taking a walk into the past when Marilyn Monroe and James Dean hypnotized the country. "I love greasy spoons," he muttered without thinking.

"Me too," Marybeth said and squeezed his hand.

A woman at the next table nodded in agreement. "I love these places too," she mumbled, gumming her pancakes to death. It was clear that privacy was one item not on the menu. The waitress returned to fill half-empty cups, forcing Kevin and Marybeth to recreate the same taste with more cream and sugar.

Within minutes, she returned with the meals. The word "enjoy," however, wasn't ten minutes old when crumpled napkins found their way into two empty plates.

While they finished off their third cups of coffee, Marybeth said, "I guess what I'm saying is, I'm not sure what I want after school, except that I don't want any more school."

He laughed and continued staring into her big chocolate eyes.

She finally stopped babbling long enough for him to lean in and kiss her.

"You're a really great listener," she said in a voice that reached just beyond a whisper, making his heart flutter. "I was thinking that I'd like to be a great listener too."

One of his eyebrows stood.

She giggled. "So the next time I see you," she said, "which I'm really looking forward to..." She gave him another kiss. "...I intend to shut my mouth and let you run with it. I'm curious about you and I'm looking forward to learning everything about you."

Kevin started to speak, but stopped. "Marybeth," he said carefully after organizing his thoughts, "you're not just a woman I know or met. You're someone I really care about...even though you want to take it slow."

"Kevin, I want to know your mind and especially your heart before we..."

He nodded. "I understand," he said. "We'll move as fast or as slow as you're comfortable with."

"Thank you for that," she whispered, hugging him.

Pushing the coffee mug away from him, Kevin said, "I'm getting together with everyone tonight." He peered hard into her eyes. "Come with me. I really want them to meet you."

She shook her head. "Not tonight," she said, "but soon."

Kevin nodded but felt confused about her reluctance to meet his friends. "Are you sure?" he asked.

"Soon," she repeated and kissed him.

He paid the tab and slid out of the booth. "Okay," he said.

She slid out of the booth behind him and grabbed his hand. "But I'd really like it if you could call me later." She looked into his eyes and smiled beautifully. "I need to hear your voice again before I go to bed."

Kevin swallowed hard and escorted her out of the greasy spoon, making room for others who salivated at the door.

~ ~ ~

Izzy, Ava, Randy and Jesse gathered on Izzy and Ava's front porch for their weekly *Thursday Night Club* get-together. As they drank beer and wine from mismatched glasses at the old wooden table—waiting on Kevin to start playing cards—they finished their discussion on the current state of the church.

"...so why is that politically incorrect?" Randy asked, grinning.

"Randy, you're beyond politically incorrect," Izzy said. "You're just incorrect."

28

Randy laughed. "And comfortable with it, you Shiite liberal," he said. "People take themselves way too seriously today." He shook his head. "I think everyone has become much too sensitive for this big bad world."

Jesse nodded. "I agree," he said, "and Randy's right. Learning morals from the church is like learning fiscal ethics from Exxon-Mobile."

At that moment, Kevin emerged from the shadows wearing a baseball helmet with a video camera duct taped to the front of it. "Quiet on the set!" he screamed.

They all laughed.

"I hope you came up with something better than that," Izzy said.

Kevin removed the ridiculous helmet and took his rightful place at the table. "Oh, I did," he said.

"Late again, Kevin?" Ava said.

He shrugged unapologetically. "I'm sure I didn't miss anything," he joked.

"It was Marybeth again, right?" Izzy commented.

He nodded.

"Why don't you just bring her along?" Ava asked.

"Yeah," Izzy said, "this isn't exactly an exclusive club."

Everyone looked at Izzy.

"Yeah, right," Kevin said and smiled. "I'll bring her around soon."

Wrapped in a heavy afghan, Ava sneezed and looked at Randy. "Can you please hand me a tissue?" she asked.

"Kiss you?" he said. "But I hardly know you."

She playfully slapped his arm. "You need better material too," she teased.

"He sure does," Kevin chimed in. "I just got his postcard from the Battleship Cove and…"

"Battleship Cove?" Izzy interrupted. "Isn't that four blocks from here?"

Randy nodded and everyone laughed. It was the perfect transition from religion to tallying the pranks and deciding the latest contest winner.

Still chuckling, Ava asked, "That's the best you can do, Randy?"

"That's exactly what I thought," Kevin blurted, smiling. "And then I figured, with amateur material like that, it has to be down to me and Jesse."

Randy stood. "I don't think so," he said excitedly.

"And why's that?" Jesse asked.

"Because Jesse was out collecting money for charity," Randy reported, nodding. "He wasn't actually pranking people."

Kevin turned to Jesse. "Be honest, how much did you collect?"

"Not even fifty bucks," Jesse said defensively, "I swear."

"Okay, so what did you do with the money?" Kevin asked.

Jesse shrugged. "I threw it into the *Wounded Warrior Project* jar at the pizza shop."

"That's it, you're disqualified," Randy said decisively.

The girls started laughing.

Jesse stood. "I'm what?"

"Randy's right," Kevin said. "You were supposed to be pranking people, not doing charity work." He grinned. "You're out of the contest, *do-gooder*."

Jesse sat back down and laughed. "Sorry guys. I guess I'll have to blame my parents. They always taught me to give more than I take."

"That's awesome," Izzy said. "How so?" she asked, clearly interested in hearing more.

Jesse smiled and his eyes grew distant. "When I was a kid, my father used to pull over for anyone who was stuck—rain, snow, it didn't matter. If someone were in need of a helping hand, he'd lend one. And there I was, in the backseat of the car, paying close attention." He smiled wide. "If parents made money raising kids, mine would have been millionaires," he added sincerely.

"Are you complementing your parents or yourself?" Randy asked.

Jesse smiled. "Both I guess. All I'm doing is pulling over and lending a hand to some folks who need it. I just hope, when I have kids, that they pay attention too."

After sneezing twice, Ava asked, "So it was your dad, then, who screwed you up and molded you into a compassionate soul?"

Jesse laughed. "Actually, my grandfather had the greatest influence on me when I was growing up. He once told me that he'd never been to a funeral where folks talked about a dead guy's bank account or the amount of houses and cars he owned. Instead, people remembered their good deeds...the help they offered others throughout their lives." Jesse paused. "Then he asked me, what if—in the end—wealth isn't defined by what we've accumulated? What if it's decided by how much we give away while we're here?"

"Your grandfather was a very wise man," Ava said, stifling a cough.

"He had his moments," Jesse said, with a loving smile. "And then there were times when he was less than appropriate."

"A Renaissance man?" Kevin asked.

Jesse chuckled. "I was seven years old when he recited a poem about a pelican to me."

"Do you remember it?" Randy asked.

Jesse cleared his throat. "A wonderful bird is the pelican. His bill will hold more than his belican. He can take in his beak. Food enough for a week. But I'm damned if I see how the helican." Jesse laughed. "At that age, I thought he was swearing."

Everyone laughed.

"Renaissance man indeed," Kevin said. After a moment, he shook his head. "You know, it's all very nice that your family taught you to be a decent guy, Jesse, but you should let them know that it just cost you seventy-five cents."

The girls continued to laugh.

"So it looks like I'm the winner then," Randy announced.

Now Kevin was on his feet. "What?"

Randy nodded, proudly. "That Big Foot prank you pulled was criminal..."

Jesse quickly jumped into the fun. "And caused great fear and..." he went wide-eyed in a pathetic display of drama, "...perhaps even suffering."

"They're right, funny man," Ava said to Kevin, turning to sneeze again.

Izzy nodded in agreement. "When the campus police siren went off, Kevin, you were disqualified right then and there," she said.

Kevin pondered this for a moment and then realized that Randy was the victor. "So you're all telling me that lame Randy wins by default?" he groaned.

As everyone nodded, Randy emptied the peanut jar and placed the three quarters into his pocket.

While the laughter continued, the five friends began to play cards—with Kevin pouting over the loss.

At the end of the night, Izzy turned to the boys. "Guys, please tell me you're not going trick-or-treating next week?"

Kevin shook his head for all three boys. "We're probably safest staying here and handing out candy this year," he said.

"Which might keep us out of jail," Jesse added.

Kevin nodded. "Yeah, Randy can dress as a scarecrow again and make more children cry."

"That was supposed to be funny," Randy said defensively.

Ava looked at them through swollen eyes and wiped her nose with another tissue. "What are you guys doing for Thanksgiving this year?" she asked.

"Going home," everyone reported.

"All except Jesse," Izzy teased. "He'll probably be dishing out mashed potatoes at the rectory kitchen again."

Jesse shook his head. "Not this year," he admitted, "although we should all head down there at some point and help them get things prepared."

"Count me in," Izzy said.

"Me too," Ava and Randy said.

Everyone looked at Kevin.

"Fine," he said, "but that'll cover me for both Thanksgiving and Christmas," he said.

Jesse shook his head at his friend. "Shame on you," he teased. "My grandfather would be very disappointed."

Kevin stood and prepared to leave for the night. "So the Renaissance man had something to say about Christmas too?"

Jesse's face turned from playful to serious. "He told me to watch how people acted toward each other around Christmas and then asked me to imagine if everyone acted that way all year long." He nodded. "I've always loved Christmas for that."

4

It was a raw autumn morning, a hard driving rain causing the air to feel ten degrees cooler than it actually was; it
was early enough that the gas-lit lamps along the buckled
sidewalk were still buzzing with a dying glow.

With his sweatshirt hood pulled down over his
head and brow, Jesse checked his watch and cringed.
Damn, I'm gonna be late, he thought. As he hurried along
to his first class, he realized that the heavy pack slung
across his shoulder wasn't helping his progress. As
he approached a crosswalk, he waited for the light to
change—and checked his watch again. Just as soon as
the light turned yellow for oncoming traffic, Jesse took
a step off the curb and—trying to time the light turning
red—started sprinting for the sidewalk across the wet,
glistening street.

A silver Lexus, speeding up to beat the red light,
raced toward the crosswalk. Jesse looked left to see the
sharp teeth of the car's front grill just inches from him.
Oh, God, he thought and as he held his breath, the car's
tires let out an eerie shriek—just before taking a hard,
mind numbing bite out of his side.

As Jesse went down, the world quickly faded to
black—and disappeared.

~ ~ ~

After squealing sideways, the car jerked to a sudden stop. An older male driver—his bloated face bleached white and showing signs of shock—jumped out of the late model Lexus and hurried to assess the damage. The young man he'd struck was lying motionless in a growing pool of blood. As several curious co-eds gathered around the gruesome scene, the driver began to panic. "Someone call an ambulance!" he yelled and looked back at the young man's bloody body. "Oh, what have I done?" The driver checked Jesse's pulse. "Oh God, no!" he screamed.

As the crowd grew thicker—with some of them becoming visibly upset—a siren wailed sorrowfully in the distance.

~ ~ ~

Across campus, Kevin was walking to class when his cell phone rang. "Not again, Randy," he said under his breath. He looked at the phone's display and nodded. "Not Randy," he confirmed and answered the call. "What's up, bro?"

Kevin listened intently for a moment. His face became distressed, until a grin appeared. "No way, bro, I'm not buying it! Jesse just lost one of our stupid contests and now he's trying to even the score."

As Kevin continued to listen, the grin was completely wiped from his face. He hung up and made a quick call. "Izzy, did you hear anything about Jesse getting hit by a car this morning?"

He listened and then shook his head. "No, me neither, but some dude from my Psych class told me that he just got messed up pretty bad over near the park on Elm. Grab Ava and meet me over there. I'll put a call into Randy." He listened again and nodded. "I know, but even if it is a hoax, I say we play along."

~ ~ ~

At the accident scene, an even larger crowd had gathered as Kevin, Randy, Izzy and Ava tried to make their way through. There were police lights—even from town—flashing. A sheet-covered stretcher was being loaded into the rear of an ambulance.

Kevin looked back at his friends and gasped. "I don't think this is a prank!"

The gang fought harder to make their way through the thick crowd. Just as the four friends got close, the ambulance doors closed and a siren howled away from the scene. With panic etched into each of their faces, they approached a police officer who was trying to keep the crowd away from the spot of the accident.

"What happened here?" Randy screamed toward him.

The police officer motioned with his palm that they remain on the sidewalk.

"Okay, okay," Randy yelled, "but tell us what happened!"

"Some kid tried to beat the light and paid for it," he said nonchalantly.

Randy looked back at his friends and then down at the street—near the area that the police officer was protecting. There was a giant red bloodstain. "Oh no..."

White-faced, Kevin grabbed a co-ed standing nearby. "Who was it?" he asked.

"Some guy named Jesse," she said. "I didn't know him."

Randy overheard this and screamed back to the police officer, "Do you think he'll be all right?"

The cop shook his head. "He was already gone by the time we got here."

"Gone?" Izzy screamed. "What?"

The police officer put his portable radio to his ear and listened. He shook his head again. "They just pronounced him dead," he reported sadly.

Ava collapsed to the sidewalk. "Please God, no! Not Jesse!" she shrieked.

Izzy and the others immediately began to mourn.

~ ~ ~

An hour later, Izzy, Ava and Kevin sat in shock on the girls' front porch. Randy slowly approached the stairs, shaking his head. His face showed every sign that he'd recently been crying.

"What—" Ava began to ask.

"—they told me that he died instantly and that..." Randy interrupted, but began crying so hard that he couldn't finish. Izzy hurried to him with a hug. "...and that he didn't feel any pain," he finished between sobs.

"Thank God for that," Kevin said, trying to be strong. "Where did they take him..." Kevin also stopped. Everyone already knew the answer.

Randy looked up from Izzy's shoulder. "The chaplain's trying to get in touch with his parents." He shook his head. "That's all I know."

"What about the driver who hit him?" Ava asked angrily.

"Yeah, he must be in custody, right?" Kevin said.

"I was wondering the same thing," Randy admitted, "so I asked." He shook his head again. "He's not."

Izzy was outraged. "He's *not?*"

Like a broken man, Randy half-shrugged. "They said it was an accident, with no alcohol or drugs involved, so he was *free to go.*"

"Free to go?" Ava repeated, more furious. "Well, good for him!"

"So what about Jesse?" Izzy whimpered. "Is he *free to go* too?" Izzy stopped, setting off a whole new round of sobbing amongst the friends.

Once they'd composed themselves, Kevin wiped his eyes and said, "You know if it was one of us behind the wheel, we'd be sitting in jail right now, charged with vehicular homicide."

"Yeah," Izzy said, "because they'd think we were texting or horsing around or on our way to some housing project to buy drugs."

Ava shook her enraged head. "Jesse's dead and he's free to go."

All four friends allowed the weight of Ava's final statement to sink in and a new round of terrible grieving began.

~ ~ ~

Jesse's funeral took place on Wednesday morning. In the cemetery, the chaplain had just finished his sermon and mourners began passing by Jesse's casket for one final good-bye.

Izzy, Ava, Kevin and Randy—each devastated—mouthed a few silent words to their deceased friend and kept right on walking until they reached a tree off in the distance.

As they sadly huddled together under the giant oak, their college professor, Professor McKee, surprised the friends by approaching them to offer her heartfelt condolences.

"Oh great," Ava said under her breath. "Look who's here."

"I'm so sorry for your loss," Professor McKee said once she reached them. "I know Jesse was a dear friend to all of you." She nodded. "He was a very special person." The heavyset woman had a mop of frizzy hair and a pair of reading glasses that sat on the bridge of a slender nose.

"He sure was," Randy agreed.

"What a waste," Izzy added angrily.

"Excuse me?" the female professor asked compassionately.

"It's a *useless* waste of life," Ava added furiously.

"Jesse's life," Kevin explained, "a life that we all know would have done some incredible things...was wasted." He took a deep breath. "All because of some stupid, random accident."

Professor McKee smiled. "You may not want to hear this right now, guys, but I don't believe there are any random acts in the universe, and nothing is done in vain—nor is anything *useless*." She searched each of their eyes. "Sometimes, you have to be patient to see how things turn out and, with any luck, reveal the *greater* purpose." She smiled gently again but—with a stern, rigid expression permanently carved into her brow—she appeared as disappointed and judgmental as ever.

This comment was immediately met with scornful glances and a few negative grunts.

"Be patient for what?" Ava asked bravely. She shook her head. "To die, so we can be with Jesse again?"

"Not at all," the woman said. "The worst thing you could ever do with your life is to wait for it to end."

"Unfortunately, Jesse didn't have that choice," Randy said. "His life was ended for him..." He wiped his eyes. "...long before it ever really began."

"I agree," the teacher said, "but you guys are still here..." She searched their eyes again. "...and you each have a choice, don't you?"

They nodded in unison.

"From where I stand, I honestly can't imagine some *great* purpose in this," Kevin admitted.

"But your perspective may change," McKee said, her tone soft. "It always does."

As more skeptical glances were exchanged between the four friends, Randy shocked them even further. "So you really believe that Jesse's life—and death—have some great purpose that we can't see?" he asked.

She nodded. "I really do. Unfortunately, people within our society believe that the person who dies with the most toys wins. For most, it's all about amassing material objects, wealth. For others, it's about compiling a list of accomplishments and accolades." She looked back toward Jesse's casket. "But have you ever been to a funeral and overheard someone praise the deceased for anything they owned?"

As their jaws dropped open, the friends listened in awe as the professor echoed Jesse's recent words—almost verbatim.

Professor McKee changed her voice to drive her point home. "Oh, what wonderful houses and cars he had!" She shook her head. "No, people are truly remembered by what they do while on this planet and, more importantly, how they help others. It's not about what you have or take, it's about what you give...and eventually leave behind." She smiled. "Imagine if we all measured wealth that way."

For the first time, the professor's words were not met with negativity. The four friends remained silent, pondering the wonderful déjà vu experience.

"What a different and glorious world this would be," Professor McKee added.

They each nodded.

"The good book says to place our treasures in heaven because that's where our hearts will be," she continued, looking toward Jesse's casket again. "It's not only a matter of faith, but the proof in your deeds." She looked back at them. "No great mystery here, guys. And I think Jesse figured it out early." She nodded. "Giving more than you take... now that's how you build a life worth living."

The friends looked at each other in awe.

With a wink, Professor McKee walked away, leaving them to internalize her lesson.

~ ~ ~

The four friends still met for the *Thursday Night Club* on Izzy and Ava's front porch. Rather than play cards, they shared bittersweet memories of Jesse.

"Who enters a best prank contest and raises money for charity?" Kevin asked, snickering. "I mean, who does that?"

"He was so amazing, wasn't he?" Izzy said. "I remember our freshman year when he helped me study for a World History test I was freaking out about. I didn't think it was a big deal until I found out he had to stay up all night to cram for his own exam that he had in the morning."

Randy shook his head. "Unreal!" he said. "Do you guys remember when Jesse couldn't make our potluck dinners last year?"

They each nodded.

"Well, I found out later he was down at the soup kitchen, volunteering." He shook his head. "When I called him on it, he asked me not to tell anyone…said that the only one who needed to know was God."

"Jesse's stories are endless," Kevin added.

"And so was his caring for other people," Ava said.

"This may sound crazy," Izzy said, "but I feel like he's still with us…sitting right here, right now."

They all agreed with solemn nods.

"Can you imagine how much good he would have done in this world had he lived a full life?" Ava suggested.

They each quietly pondered this for a few minutes. Suddenly, Izzy became excited. "What if, in Jesse's memory, we have another contest…" she said, thinking aloud, "…only this time, whoever pulls off the greatest or kindest deed, wins the pot?"

Each of them considered this for a brief moment and smiled.

Grinning, Ava grabbed the empty jar and dropped the first quarter into it. The others reached into their pockets and did the same. Randy came up empty and turned to Kevin. "I need to borrow a quarter, bro," he said quietly.

Kevin handed it to him and Randy dropped in the last coin.

"The rules?" Kevin asked.

"It must be anonymous," Izzy said, "just like Jesse would have wanted. Only the four of us…" She stopped to think briefly before continuing, "…and Professor McKee can know about what we've done."

They each smiled in agreement.

"And we have until midnight on Christmas—" Randy said.

"—in memory of Jesse's favorite holiday," Ava interrupted.

"Perfect," Izzy muttered.

Again, they each agreed.

"The kind act cannot cost money," Ava added.

"Our own money, you mean?" Kevin interrupted. "We should be allowed to get others to donate, right?"

Ava nodded. They each followed suit.

"Okay then," Izzy said, "let's go honor Jesse."

"...and win a whole dollar," Randy joked.

"...and maybe four lives worth living," Ava concluded.

~ ~ ~

The following day, the four friends met Professor McKee on the quad and let her in on their plan.

With a proud smile, she nodded. "I honestly can't think of a better way to honor the memory of a friend," she said. "And if you ask me, Jesse's still giving, isn't he?"

Each set of eyes filled with tears.

5

Although the four friends expected to begin their inspired quests with a bang, the chaos of daily college life consumed them. Potluck dinners of English muffin pizzas and Ramen noodles were devoured while cramming for exams and running off to part-time jobs on campus to offset expenses. Even still, there were some good deeds performed.

Ava started writing letters, recruiting people to prepare Christmas cards to soldiers overseas, while Randy opted to sit back and not rush into anything. Izzy began volunteering at the local elementary school, reading to children—where she learned about the high rate of illiteracy and the severe lack of books in the community.

As the winds picked up, leaves of fire engine red and pumpkin orange lost their luster and floated to the ground, creating a temporary rainbow blanket—before decomposing and becoming one with the earth again. Kevin got a jump on winter by passing out hand warmers and socks to the homeless. Those who panhandled on the corner wearing gold jewelry, though, received nothing.

~ ~ ~

As the weather grew colder and the four co-eds settled into their busy routines, the need to lend a helping hand in Jesse's name became a priority.

Oak and maple skeletons—stripped completely bare of their colorful clothing—lined the desolate street. It was just getting dark when Kevin turned up his collar against a sudden chill and took a seat beside one of his homeless friends.

"Here you go, Gus," Kevin said, handing the grinning man a clean pair of socks and a blanket.

"Thank you," Gus replied, his tone humble.

"My pleasure," Kevin said, "but I could also use your help."

"Name it," Gus said.

"I think I've finally met *the one*," Kevin said, "but she's confusing the hell out of me. Every time I think I know how to act, I'm wrong. Every time I think I've reacted correctly, I'm wrong. I mean…just the other night I noticed she had a tone that made her sound unsure of me. I wouldn't ask if it didn't mean so much to me."

"Ahhh," Gus sighed and as he searched his memory, his tired eyes sparkled. "Women can be a rough trip, but there's no better ride on earth."

Kevin matched the man's sigh in agreement.

Gus thought about it for an extended moment and shook his head. "Women are creatures of the heart, Kevin. They don't want to be understood…just loved." He grinned. "But what a wasted life, my boy, to never know their ways."

"I hear that," Kevin whispered and searched his friend's face. "Sounds like you've had some experience with this subject?"

Gus's eyes flickered again. "I didn't always live on the streets, Kevin," he said. "There was a time..."

"Good for you," Kevin whispered.

Gus nodded and, although he clearly gave the matter some serious thought, he was at a loss for words. "Kevin, as we sit here, it's become clear to me that I know as much about women as any other guy." He shrugged. "Which is very little." He put his hand on Kevin's shoulder. "So it looks like the rest becomes your research project. Trust me, son, if this girl is *the one*, your assignment will last a lifetime."

"Thanks, Gus."

He squeezed Kevin's shoulder. "Hey, when and *if* you do find some answers, let me know. I've always been just as curious." He winked.

Kevin laughed. As he stood, he reached into his pocket and retrieved a gift card to a local fast food restaurant. "Dinner's on me, my friend," he said before walking off into the shadows of the night.

~ ~ ~

In the morning, Izzy sat in the local hospital's waiting room, filling in the last few details on a donor's application. After checking it over, she submitted it. Within minutes, her mouth was swabbed and she was added to the *Be The Match Registry* for bone marrow donors.

"If you match a patient," Rhonda, the smiling nurse, explained, "we'll contact you to see if you're still willing to donate. If you agree to proceed, we'll ask you about your health to be sure it's safe for you to donate bone marrow. Then we'll schedule more testing to see if you're the best match for the patient. Throughout this process, you're likely to be one of several people being tested. The chance of being selected is about one in twelve."

"Sounds easy enough," Izzy said.

Rhonda nodded. "You may be contacted at different stages of the patient's matching process. When you're ranked high on a list as a possible match for a patient, a doctor may request additional testing to help narrow the list of potential donors." She smiled.

"I understand," Izzy said.

"At that point," Rhonda added, "we'll answer all of your questions...which everyone has. It can sometimes take up to two months for the patient's doctor to get the testing results and select a donor. The patient's condition also affects the timing. And we'd keep you posted on the doctor's decision." Rhonda placed Izzy's sample into a kit.

"Great!" Izzy said.

"Any questions?"

Izzy pointed to the swab kit. "Is that it for today?" she asked.

Rhonda nodded. "If we need more, we'll be in touch." She smiled and rolled her eyes for effect. "Trust me."

With a final nod, Izzy left.

~ ~ ~

Four blocks over at the Rolling Hills Retirement Home, Ava was interviewing for a volunteer's position with Mrs. Deborah Sullivan, the retirement home's director. "I'd like to volunteer some time at your home and help," Ava told the woman.

"Well, we can never have too much of that," Mrs. Sullivan said with a smile.

"Where could you use me the most?" Ava asked. "Washing dishes? Running errands?"

"Actually, spending time with our residents is what we most need."

"Spending time?" Ava repeated. "Doing what?"

Mrs. Sullivan looked into her eyes. "Talking, watching TV, playing cards..." she shrugged, "...hopefully laughing."

"And that would make the most difference?" Ava asked.

"Oh, more than you could ever imagine, Ava," Mrs. Sullivan explained. "Many of these people have been forgotten, cast aside by more important priorities in their families' lives. Many are near the end of their lives and...well, they're alone. I can't imagine anything sadder than that."

"Me either," Ava said.

"Yes, it's terrible. Our society has forgotten the value in their wisdom and everything they've done to make our lives better than what they lived."

"Then count me in," Ava said excitedly. "I'd love to spend some of my time with them."

"You won't regret it. I promise," the older woman said. "And don't be surprised if you end up getting more out of it than you put in."

"I'm not looking for anything in return," Ava said.

"I realize that, but it's inevitable. You'll see." She smiled. "So can you come back later in the week to meet our cast of characters?"

"Absolutely," Ava said, "I can be here on Friday at three o'clock, right after my last class."

~ ~ ~

On a sidewalk near the college, Kevin was tacking up flyers that read, *Riding for Higher Education*.

"What's that all about?" some passerby asked.

Kevin revealed a pledge sheet. "I'm soliciting donations for a fundraiser I'm running. I'm gonna ride from Boston to the tip of Cape Cod to raise enough money to start a scholarship."

"Wish I'd thought of that when I went to college," the stranger joked.

Kevin chuckled. "Actually, it's not for me. I'm graduating this year. No, the money will be going to some high school kid who would never have a shot at college otherwise."

"That's awesome," the passerby said. Waving off the pledge sheet, he dug into his pocket, pulled out a twenty-dollar bill and handed it to Kevin. "Well, here's my donation. Good luck."

As Kevin watched the man walk away, he smiled. *Not a bad start*, he thought and finished nailing up his flyer.

~ ~ ~

Randy sat alone in the cafeteria, holding a thick Italian sub and gazing out the window. *I wonder whether Kevin, Ava and Izzy have already gotten started*, he thought. He shrugged to himself and took a bite of his overstuffed sandwich. *Ahh, it doesn't matter. I've got time*, he thought. *Plenty of time.* He tore another chunk out of his sandwich and returned his attention to the window—where he could stare off into nothingness.

~ ~ ~

The four friends gathered for their weekly get-together on the front porch.

It was a quiet night with some small talk. Finally, Izzy asked what they were all wondering. "Well, is anyone going to update the group on their progress?"

Each one of them shook his or her head.

Ava laughed. "Are you, Iz?" she asked.

Izzy grinned. "Heck, no!"

Kevin looked at Randy. "You probably haven't even started yet, right?" he teased.

"Sure, I have," Randy said, "I've made up my mind to make a positive difference." He smirked.

"Okay, but have you made any effort to—"

"—to chase something down?" Randy interrupted. "No! I have a strong sense that my good deeds will pick me...and I'll know them exactly when I see them."

"In other words," Ava said, "you're *lazy*."

They all laughed and began playing cards.

6

On Friday afternoon, Mrs. Sullivan caught Ava in the Rolling Hills Retirement Home courtyard. "How's it going?" she asked.

"Great!" Ava said, smiling. "I love it."

Mrs. Sullivan nodded. "Wonderful!" She then pointed to an old lady sitting alone. "Have you spent any time with our elder stateswoman, Mrs. LeComte, yet?"

Ava shook her head.

"When you get a chance, check in on her," Mrs. Sullivan suggested. "She can't remember to take her medication and couldn't tell you what she had for breakfast, but just ask her anything about her life..." she grinned, "...and see what happens."

Ava smiled. "I will."

Mrs. Sullivan winked at her. "Just make sure you have some time to spend with her before you ask, because she can talk."

~ ~ ~

Moments later, Ava walked over to check in on Mrs. LeComte and introduce herself. The ancient woman was sitting in a wheelchair—wrapped in a thick blanket—in a quiet corner of the yard. As Ava approached her, she extended her hand. "Hello, Mrs. LeComte. I'm Ava. Is it okay if I sit with you for a bit?"

Mrs. LeComte smiled and gestured with her hand that Ava take a seat on the bench beside her. "Oh, that would be lovely, sweetheart," she said in a soft, raspy voice. She looked up at the sky. "The good Lord's seen fit to give us another beautiful day, hasn't he?"

Ava nodded. "He sure has."

They sat quietly for a few moments; Mrs. LeComte seemingly at ease with the company, Ava feeling awkward with the extended silence.

"So I'm told that you've lived quite a life?" Ava said, fighting against the silence.

Mrs. LeComte grinned. "Almost two of them by now," she joked.

Ava smiled and, without thinking, shuffled down the bench to get even closer to the pleasant woman.

"I was born in Fall River, Massachusetts on the twelfth of May." She squinted, peering into Ava's attentive eyes. "And Fall River was the place to be when the textile industry was in its heyday."

"Fall River?" Ava repeated, smirking. "Isn't that where Lizzie Borden took an axe—"

"—and gave her father forty whacks," the old woman added, finishing the rhyme. "When she saw what she had done, she gave her mother forty one."

Ava laughed. "So do you think the axe was hers?"

Mrs. LeComte half-shrugged. "Could have been," she said and then grinned. "Women worked just as hard as men in those days."

Ava laughed harder.

Mrs. LeComte smiled, her old eyes filled with mischief. "You know, I've lived long enough to meet five generations of my family and I have forty grandchildren," she said.

"Wow, that's amazing!"

The old woman nodded, proudly. "I was thirty years old when I got married, which was an old spinster in those days. We met at the North End Laundry which was right on the banks of the Taunton River." Her eyes grew distant in memory and she chuckled. "In the winter, I had to strap on my skates and commute to work across the river." She nodded. "We had five children—four boys and one girl. Then, my Robert passed on from a bad ticker, leaving me to raise all five kids during the Great Depression." She looked into Ava's eyes again and smirked playfully. "Not very considerate of him, if you ask me."

"That must have been a lot of work?" Ava said, ignoring the witty comment.

"We worked hard back then and we went to church every Sunday," Mrs. LeComte continued. "It was a simpler time, I think. That is, until the hurricane of 1938 wiped out the old laundry. From then on, I traveled the trolleys and took on whatever odd jobs I could find."

Ava was hypnotized by the elder's vivid tales.

"When World War II hit, two of my boys joined the Coast Guard, while the other two chose the Army Air Corps. For years, I had four stars hanging in my front window, one for each of 'em." She shook her head. "While they were off fighting, though I didn't have much I volunteered my time." She patted Ava's knee. "Just like you." She stared off for a moment, trying to picture something in her mind. "Sometimes, I even made up food baskets for the needy."

Ava's eyes lit up as she considered the new idea.

"Thankfully, all my boys made it back," the old woman reported. "It wasn't long after that I got involved in the American Legion and wouldn't you know it, I became the first woman president of the local AMVETS."

"Wow!" Ava said again.

"Through the years," she continued with distant eyes, "life went on and I got a second chance at love." She nodded. "Yup, I married William Benoit and after three happy years, a heart attack took him too. I've sometimes wondered whether I killed them both." She winked at Ava again. "I must have been too much to handle back then."

Ava laughed hard—from her belly. *It's the first time I've laughed since Jesse died,* she realized.

"Right after Bill died, I bought my first car, a used Hudson Terraplane. And if I wasn't out driving, then I was sitting in the backyard, watching the steamboats paddle down river. I always loved that."

"You really have lived an amazing life, Mrs. LeComte," Ava sighed.

The old lady nodded. "I've seen more American presidents than I care to count, come and go...all this country's wars, Prohibition, the Great Depression, and the Civil Rights Movement, which was nothing compared to the day-to-day troubles that we had to overcome." She searched Ava's eyes. "If life is a test of endurance, then I think I've passed the test." She paused and then whispered, "But it's not, you know."

"Not what?" Ava asked.

"A test of endurance. Nope, life is just a never-ending series of choices." She nodded. "So make sure you choose to be happy every chance you get, okay?"

"I will," Ava promised and then sat for a few more moments in silence. This time, it felt comfortable. As she got up to leave, she told the wise old soul, "It was wonderful meeting you, Mrs. LeComte."

"You too, dear."

"Be sure to take your pills, okay?" Ava reminded her.

"What day is it?" Mrs. LeComte asked, confused.

"It's Tuesday."

"And I need to take my pills on Tuesday?"

"You do," Ava said with a smile. "You need to take them every day, Mrs. LeComte."

~ ~ ~

Exactly one week from the day she'd completed the bone marrow donation application, Izzy was sitting on a bench in the middle of the campus quad, studying alone. Her cell phone rang and she picked it up. "Hello," she said, listening. "Are you kidding me? Already? That's great!" She cringed. "Well, I don't mean that it's *great*, but..." She listened more. "Of course I'm still interested in donating. When do you need me to come in?" She nodded. "I'll be there."

Izzy hung up the phone and sat on the bench for a while, thinking, *I hope you're with me on this, Jesse, 'cause I'm scared to do it alone.*

~ ~ ~

Across town on the campus quad, Kevin and Randy were also sitting on a bench. They were studying together when two college kids—Rachel and Jonathan—approached.

"So what's up with this bike-a-thon to the Cape?" Jonathan asked. "It's getting a little late in the season for a ride, isn't it?"

Kevin put his book down and grinned. "Not really," he said. "Besides, it's only a four day trek, a hundred sixty miles round-trip. I'll camp out at night and ride hard during the day. I'll be heading out in two weeks..." he smiled again, "...as long as we don't get an early snow."

Everyone laughed.

"What's the scholarship called that you're raising money for?" Rachel asked.

"It's called, *A Hand Up*," Kevin replied.

"Very cool," Jonathan said. "Where do we sign up?"

Kevin quickly reached into his book bag for his pledge sheets.

Rachel and Jonathan saw this and laughed. "No," Rachel said, "we want to ride with you."

"You what?" Kevin asked, confused.

"Where do we sign up to ride with you?" Jonathan asked, jumping in.

Kevin thought about this for a few moments and smiled to himself. *I hadn't even considered getting other people to ride with me,* he thought and stood. "Consider yourself signed up." He paused. "It might be cold on the road though."

"Not for real riders," Rachel said smirking.

"But you'll need to raise money in order to ride," Kevin added.

"Of course," Jonathan said. "How much?"

"Two hundred fifty dollars each," he said hesitantly.

Rachel sighed. "Great," she said, "I thought it would be more. Do you have pledge forms we can use?"

Kevin handed them a blank pledge sheet. "I only have this one. Do you mind making copies?"

Jonathan shook his head. "Not at all." As he and Rachel began walking away, Jonathan stopped and turned around. "Oh Kevin, the guys from the lacrosse team are interested in riding too. They said they can incorporate it into their training, while helping some poor schmuck get into school." He chuckled, joking, "But you might want to catch them before they sober up and change their minds."

Kevin nodded and took a seat, dumbfounded.

Watching this, Randy started to laugh and patted his back. "Looks like the train has left the station and there's no turning back now," he said nodding. "Good for you, Kev."

Kevin smiled wide, quickly throwing all of his stuff into his backpack and standing up again. "I've got to go and make some new fliers..." he nodded, "...and pledge forms. Looks like I've got some recruiting to do."

~ ~ ~

Overwhelmed with excitement, Kevin filled Marybeth in on every detail of his charitable plan. While he rambled on, she sat in silence—her right eyebrow raised in skepticism. "What?" he finally asked, surprised by her frigid reaction. "You don't think it's a good idea?"

"I don't know," she said. "The whole thing seems really time consuming to me." She shook her head. "Besides, I think people should pay their own way and not expect a hand-out."

The air left Kevin's lungs and he suddenly felt lightheaded. "But it's not a hand out," he muttered, "it's..." He halted the explanation. The initial sting he'd felt was veering away from hurt and heading down the road toward anger. "How have you paid for school, Marybeth?" he asked, trying to keep his voice even.

"My parents," she answered nonchalantly.

Kevin felt his heart sink. *Marybeth's not who I thought she was*, he realized and stood to leave.

"Where are you going?" she asked, oblivious to their relationship-ending exchange.

He sighed sadly. "I need to go waste my time helping people," he said and walked away.

~ ~ ~

Rhonda met Izzy in the hospital waiting room. They shook hands. "That didn't take long," Izzy teased.

"Which tells me that there are no other matches," Rhonda said, "or very few." She smiled. "If I had to guess, somebody's been waiting *just for you*...and needs you right now."

"I'm sorry I didn't sign up sooner," Izzy said.

Rhonda shook her head. "Not at all. You signed up exactly when you should have." She handed Izzy some paperwork. "Today, you'll be participating in an information session, where we'll give you detailed information about the donation and recovery process, including all the risks and side effects. If you still agree to donate, we'll need you to sign a consent form."

"No problem," Izzy said.

"Next, we'll give you a thorough physical exam to make sure your donation is safe for both you and the patient."

Izzy nodded. "Let's do it," she said with determination.

"Okay then," Rhonda said and led her down the long, sanitized hall.

~ ~ ~

On Thursday night, the four friends gathered for their weekly get-together.

"You're never going to bring Marybeth by here to meet us, are you?" Izzy said to Kevin.

He shook his head. "Nope. I'm not." His eyes were filled with anger and sorrow.

Looks were exchanged around the table but nobody questioned it further.

Quickly changing the subject, Ava turned to Randy. "Still nothing, slacker?" she asked.

Randy smiled and shook his head. "Look, I have a pretty good idea about Kevin's plan..."

Kevin placed his pointer finger to his lips, halting any further details from his big-mouthed friend.

Randy nodded. "And God only knows what you girls have cooked up, but when I find my moment," he said, grinning, "I promise it'll be amazing!"

"Do you think that moment might come before Christmas night?" Izzy teased.

"Does it matter?" Randy asked seriously.

They all considered this and shook their heads.

"In the bigger picture, I guess it really doesn't matter," Ava said.

7

A few short days had passed when Rhonda approached Izzy in the hospital waiting room. "Okay, I called you to come in because the tests are already back from the lab," she said.

Izzy nodded. "You guys are quick, aren't you?"

Rhonda's face turned serious. "In this case, we have no choice." She put her hand on Izzy' shoulder. "Izzy, you're the most suitable donor and you're being asked to donate right away."

"When?" Izzy asked nervously.

"Today." Rhonda searched her eyes, hopefully. "Is that possible?"

Izzy nodded. "I can't think of one thing that's more important."

Rhonda sighed, relieved. "I think you're right," she said and then led her away again—her pace now urgent.

~ ~ ~

On the campus quad, a local newspaper reporter interviewed Kevin about his fundraising efforts for *A Hand Up* scholarship. "What's your goal?" the reporter asked.

"Eleven thousand five hundred dollars or enough to cover a full year's tuition," Kevin said.

"Great. Do you think you'll make it?"

"It'll be close," Kevin admitted. "So far, we've had lots of pledges, but most are from students who attend this school—people who don't have a lot of money to spare."

"And the faculty?" the reporter asked, "have they been supportive?"

"They have, but we still need all the help we can get." He paused. "That's why I'm so grateful you agreed to run our story in the paper."

The reporter nodded. "Hopefully, you'll get some local business support once the piece runs next week."

Kevin was surprised. "Wow, I hadn't even thought about that."

The news reporter nodded. "Oh yeah, that's where the real money is, especially if this is going to be an annual scholarship."

Kevin was taken aback again and the reporter caught it. He took a break from writing. "It is going to be an annual scholarship, isn't it?"

Kevin half-shrugged. "I guess it could be."

"You have a much better chance of corporate funding or local business support if this isn't a one-shot deal."

Kevin nodded. "It'll be annual," he said.

The reporter smiled and wrote furiously into his notebook. Upon closing the pad, he extended his hand to Kevin. "Good luck with all of this. It's a great cause. And I have to imagine that there'll be a lot more folks stepping up to offer their support." He tapped on his notepad and grinned. "At least if I have my say."

"I can't thank you enough," Kevin said.

"No," the newsman said, "thank you, Kevin."

~ ~ ~

Dressed in a hospital gown, Izzy lay on a gurney—a doctor preparing her for the outpatient procedure. "Donating marrow is a life-saving gift," the medicine man said, "so thank you for volunteering."

Izzy nodded.

"In a few minutes, you'll receive anesthesia, so obviously you'll feel no pain," the doctor said. "Once you're asleep, I'll use a needle to withdraw liquid marrow from the back of your pelvic bone. The marrow will completely replace itself within four to six weeks. Recovery times vary depending on the individual and most donors are able to return to work, school, and other activities within one to seven days after the donation procedure." He paused. "You can expect to feel some soreness in your lower back for a few days and possibly longer. Most marrow donors report that they feel completely recovered within three weeks, but we'll follow up with you until you're able to resume normal activity. Okay?"

"Okay," Izzy said.

"No need to be nervous," he said with a gentle smile.

"I'm not," Izzy said honestly. "I have a friend looking over me."

The doctor nodded—as if he understood—and gestured that the orderlies wheel her into surgery.

~ ~ ~

It was dusk. After being driven home by the same car service that had transported her to the hospital, Izzy was sitting on the porch, wrapped in a blanket. When Ava came home, she saw that Izzy looked quite ill and began to question her. "Where the heck have you been all day?"

"I went to the doctor's," Izzy said. "I haven't been feeling well. I must have spent three hours in the waiting room."

"Why didn't you call me?" Ava asked, concerned. "I could have...

"Wasted your whole day too?" Izzy interrupted. "No, I don't think so."

"So what did the doctor say?" Ava asked.

Izzy avoided her friend's eyes. "They're not sure yet. They think it might be mono. The blood tests will take a day or two." It was only a white lie, but it still bothered her to tell it.

"Oh, Iz. Is there anything I can do?"

Izzy smiled. "No thanks. I'm just achy, that's all. I'm sure I'll be okay in a few days."

Ava stood and headed for the house: "I'll go make you a cup of tea." She stopped at the door. "And I'll do whatever you need for the book drive you're putting together. It's the least I can do." She winked. "It won't even count toward the contest."

"Thanks, Ava."

"I'll call the boys later to let them know there's no get-together this week. You need to rest."

"Perfect," Izzy said, relieved. "Thanks."

~ ~ ~

The following day, after tending to Izzy, Ava reported to Rolling Hills to spend time with one of the residents, Mrs. Oliveira.

"I try to be nice to everyone," Ava said. "Everyone's fighting some battle."

Mrs. Oliveira grinned. "My grandfather used to say the same exact thing." For a moment, her eyes grew distant. "He was a quiet old fisherman—always out to sea from sun up 'til sun down—fishing." She shook her head slightly. "One day, he arrived home much earlier than usual. He took a shower and clipped his fingernails, which was unusual for him. He dressed in the same suit he'd gotten married in and walked out to the backyard where he sat alone under his grape vines." She looked at Ava. "My grandmother thought the old salt had finally lost his marbles...but twenty minutes later she found him dead."

"Oh, I'm sorry," Ava blurted, surprised by the story's ending.

Mrs. Oliveira shook her head again. "Oh don't be, sweetheart. It's the natural course of things." She half-shrugged. "He got cleaned up to go home and that's all there was to it." Her smile reappeared. "I'm looking forward to seeing him again," she whispered.

After a moment, Ava felt the need to break the awkward silence. "I really love spending time here," she told Mrs. Oliveira.

The old woman's eyes returned to the present and she placed her full attention on Ava once again. "It shows," the old woman said.

"I can't explain it," Ava said, "but all my worries seem to melt away when I walk through the front door."

"That's what happens when you're thinking about other people," Mrs. Oliveira said. "There's no time to dwell on your own troubles." She smiled. "I guess that's the gift you give yourself when you're helping others?"

"Must be," Ava said. "All I know is that I really love being here."

"Rolling Hills isn't the perfect place, but most of us are lucky to be here. At least we have each other..." she grabbed Ava's hand, "...and kind souls like you who come to visit."

"It could always be worse, right?" Ava said.

"There were never truer words spoken, sweetheart. Many folks my age are shut-ins, living alone with little to eat and no one to care for them."

"Do you know of any I could look in after?" Ava asked.

The woman smiled wide. "You're on a real mission, Ava, aren't you?" Mrs. Oliveira asked.

Ava returned the smile. "Yeah, you could say that."

~ ~ ~

It was dusk at a local café. Kevin was meeting with Mr. Sweeney, a local businessman, who wanted to discuss the possibility of offering support to *A Hand Up* scholarship.

"Thanks so much for taking the time to meet with me," Kevin said. "I really appreciate it."

"My pleasure, Kevin. I'm excited for the opportunity to get involved," the man said with a grin. "To be honest, without scholarship money I would have spent my entire life working in the same factory my father slaved in for forty years. But thanks to that college education, I now own the building."

"That's great," Kevin said and then felt nervous. "So tell me, how can I get you behind this annual scholarship?"

"I only have one question," Mrs. Sweeney said. "What are the requirements to receive the scholarship?"

"There will be three criteria," Kevin said, counting on his fingers. "Good grades, which proves a real value of education." He paused. "An essay, answering one question: Tell us what you've done for someone other than yourself."

"But that's only two," Mr. Sweeney said.

"Oh, and you must be able to ride a bike," Kevin added, smiling, "and be willing to pay it forward."

"Say no more, Kevin. Put my company down for five thousand dollars a year."

Kevin sat in shock.

Mr. Sweeney smiled, picked up a menu and asked, "So how are the burgers here?"

~ ~ ~

It was just past twilight on the campus. Randy was walking through the quad when he spotted a suspicious-looking silhouette of a man standing in one of the building's shadows. Randy slowed down and watched the guy—who was trying to be inconspicuous—clearly eyeing a girl who was sitting alone. Randy stepped into the shadows of a building across from them and after ensuring that he could not be seen, took out his cell phone and continued watching.

The girl was oblivious to the creepy shadow watching her. Randy looked around and discovered that the campus was now completely desolate of other people. The girl eventually got up, put her backpack over her shoulder and started walking toward the parking lot. As she passed the predator, he remained in the shadows. She got another twenty feet when the man emerged and began to slowly follow her.

"Oh boy," Randy said under his breath and stepped out of the shadows to discreetly follow the girl and her stalker. As Randy walked, he called the campus police station. "You need to dispatch a car to the east parking lot," he whispered. "It looks like some girl's in trouble." He listened. "It doesn't matter who I am. Just get someone over there right now."

As the girl reached the darkened parking lot, the stalker picked up his pace. Randy dropped his backpack onto the ground and started jogging. "Here we go," he muttered under his breath, steeling himself for the inevitable confrontation.

The stalker grabbed the girl by the arm and violently pulled her down. The girl screamed out. A few seconds later, Randy was upon them both and tackled the potential sex offender. While the man struggled, Randy pinned the animal's arms behind his back and made him scream out in pain. Randy then sat atop the assailant, completely immobilizing him. "I've fought guys tougher than you and most were tougher than me," he panted and then leaned into the squirming man's ear. "Keep struggling and I'll break your arm, I swear it."

The man immediately lay still in the prone position.

Randy looked over at the girl, who was clearly in shock. "Call nine-one-one," he told her. "By the time the campus police get here..."

Just then, the campus police car's siren called out in the distance. The girl looked at Randy.

"Make the call," he barked at her, trying to pull her from her shock.

The girl finished the 911 call just as the campus police responded to the scene of the attempted rape. The officer jumped out of his cruiser and approached.

"Get some cuffs on this scum bag!" Randy told him. "He just attacked this girl."

The campus cop turned to the girl. "Is that true?" he asked.

By now, she was crying and trembling. "Yes," she whimpered, "he pulled me down and…and was trying to get my pants off when this man tackled him." She began crying harder. "Oh…thank…God," she stuttered, her body convulsing.

The campus cop quickly retrieved his handcuffs. Randy helped him apply the restraints before climbing off the sex offender.

"This is crap!" the sex offender complained. "I didn't do anything."

The campus policeman shined a flashlight in the sex offender's face.

"Save it," he barked. "Your photo's been hanging in our station for the past two years."

Another siren screamed in the distance. A local police car was responding to the scene. Randy winked at the girl and turned to leave.

"Hey, you're not going anywhere," the campus cop told Randy. "We need you to…"

Ignoring the man, Randy started walking away. "Can't chief," he told the man, "it's past my bedtime. Besides, it was all you."

"Hey, stop," the campus policeman called out again.

Randy ran off into the darkness and grabbed his backpack before being swallowed by the night.

8

Some long, hard weeks had passed, weeks filled with mourning and terrible grief, blanketed in seriousness and some heavy responsibilities. *How would Jesse lighten things up?* Kevin wondered and smiled. *I know exactly how.* Right or wrong, Kevin decided it was time for some much needed comic relief.

Thursday morning rolled around. With a yawn, Kevin looked at his alarm clock. It read 6:55 *a.m.* He smiled. *Time to get up*, he thought and swung his feet onto the floor. For a moment, the short stocky man peered out his bedroom window. It was another late fall morning—most of the world gray and preparing for a long hibernation. He looked back at his alarm clock and felt a rush of excitement. *Oh crap*, he thought, *they said seven o'clock.*

He quietly maneuvered past three piles of laundry—clean, clean enough and don't even think about putting it on again until it's washed—and stepped into the sparsely furnished living room. He turned on the radio—to low—and began flipping through the channels. From songs to talk shows, his hand moved quickly, searching for the right station. Suddenly, he found it through the static and stopped. Taking a seat on the edge of the worn leather sofa, he smiled and listened.

Randy's—his roommate's—cell phone started singing in the other room. Several seconds later, a telephone began ringing on the radio. Kevin smiled wider.

Randy answered, "Hello?" He was obviously half-asleep.

"Hi," the morning DJ said, "may I speak with Randy Duhon please?"

"Yeah, this is Randy."

"Randy, DJ Ramone here from Groovin' 92.8."

"Oh, hey Ramone," Randy said; he was excited and completely awake now.

Kevin heard movement in the other room and chuckled.

"Randy, I have your resumé here in front of me and was wondering if I could take a few minutes of your time this morning to interview you?" DJ Ramone said. "In radio, there's no better way to measure a person's talents than through good old fashioned improv. Sound good?"

"Sounds real good," Randy said, his voice clearly nervous. "Let's do it!"

Kevin chuckled more.

"Great," the DJ said, "well, it says here that you're interested in a DJ internship with 92.8?"

"Absolutely! And I'd work hard for you too!" Randy vowed.

"Excellent. That's just what we want to hear." There was a pause. "And it just so happens that we might have an opening real soon."

"Seriously?" Randy said. "Wow, that's awesome!"

There was a bang in Randy's bedroom. *He dropped his phone*, Kevin thought, smiling, and listened as his friend scrambled to pick it up.

"Sure is and it might be a great opportunity for someone with your aspirations," the DJ added. "The thing is, though, the show's executive producer has his heart set on finding a young British intern or at least someone who can pull off the accent. Still interested?"

Randy hesitated. "Did you say you want someone with a British accent?" he asked.

"I did," the disc jockey confirmed. "Are you still in?"

"Ugh...yeah, sure," Randy said, baffled.

Kevin stifled a chuckle that quickly turned into a giggle.

"Trust me, Randy. I've been in this business a long time and this is exactly the kind of thing that'll take off," DJ Ramone said. "I can almost guarantee you that the *Rockin' Randy Show* will be a big hit! How 'bout we run through some dialogue right now? You up for it?"

"I sure am. Let's do it!"

Kevin could hear his roommate pacing the floor now.

"Okay, so let's hear your intro," the DJ said.

There was a brief pause. Then, as thousands of morning commuters listened in, Randy turned on his best British accent and sold his soul for a radio job. "Hey, hey, hey, it's Rockin' Randy," he said in an absolutely terrible accent that sounded more like Australian with a mix of Mandarin Chinese, "and I'm comin' your way, so if you wanna play you'd better stay...on Groovin' 92.8!"

"Wow. Nice job!" DJ Ramone said, acting impressed. He then deepened his voice, pretending to interview him. "So, Rockin' Randy, how's life been treating you since you landed in the States?"

"I have to tell you, Ramone," Randy said in the awful accent, "back in my old flat, I had my worries... really got my knickers in a twist about not fittin' in, you know? But you Yanks have been first rate. I wouldn't take a thousand quid to go back." He sighed heavily. "Aye, this is home now."

Kevin laughed so hard into the sofa pillow that he began to cry.

Ramone was also clearly enjoying the prank. "But you must miss some things about good old England?" he asked.

"Sure, I miss me Mum's bangers and mash," Randy replied, the accent getting even worse. "There's no lift in the flat I moved into, so I have to take the stairs..." He took a deep breath, which sounded like a nervous wheeze. "And I'm still trying to figure out how to work the loo over here."

With laughter creeping into his voice, DJ Ramone didn't miss a beat and kept the fake interview moving along. "So tell me, any hobbies, Rockin' Randy?"

"I play cricket when I'm not spinnin' records, you know?"

"I do, except we haven't actually *spun* records in the States for a few years now."

Randy was stumped. Finally, he muttered, "Right oh, I knew that."

"Did you get your own wheels yet or are you taking the bus?" DJ Ramone asked him.

"I did purchase a moto car," Randy said, sounding like a chipmunk on steroids, "but the first time I lifted the bonnet to top off, I was surprised to discover that the petrol tank was located near the boot." He thought for a moment. "And when the windscreen got dirty, I..."

DJ Ramone began to laugh, halting Randy's horrendous spiel.

While the morning host struggled to get out another question, Kevin was rolling around on the couch, trembling in hysterics.

"Wow, that must have been quite the discovery," DJ Ramone finally managed. "Well, *we've* got a little surprise for you today, too, Rockin' Randy."

"Cheers, mate! I fancy surprises, I do," he said, still pacing nervously behind the closed door.

Ramone laughed. "That's good," he said, "because, Rockin' Randy, you've just been *scammed*."

There was a moment of silence. Even the pacing stopped.

"Pardon me?" Randy said, still staying with the bad accent.

"Kevin told us that you're a communications major at the college and would do anything to work in radio," Ramone explained.

"Good God, no!" Randy yelled in his normal voice—which Kevin heard twice; once from the other room and the second time on the delayed radio program.

DJ Ramone laughed. "And he wasn't lying, was he?"

"Oh man, he's *so* dead," Randy barked even louder before hanging up the phone and throwing open his bedroom door.

As the music played at the end of the scam, Kevin sprinted for their bathroom. He quickly locked the door behind him and hyperventilated from laughter. "Gotcha buddy," he said through the door.

Randy let out a wounded grunt and stomped back to his room, where he nearly slammed the door off its hinges.

Kevin unlocked the bathroom door and cautiously peeked out. "Gotcha," he repeated.

~ ~ ~

Thursday finally arrived and the four friends got together on Izzy and Ava's front porch.

"So, Rockin' Randy, when do you start your new job at the radio station?" Ava asked, starting the night with the usual banter.

Both Izzy and Kevin laughed.

"Real funny," Randy said, looking wounded. "I thought we were supposed to be helping people, not hurting them?"

"Oh please!" Izzy said. "Don't be so dramatic."

Unable to hold back, Randy cracked a smile.

Ava shook her head. "It was the first time I've laughed since Jesse died."

"Me too," Izzy said. "And it was the first time things felt like they used to."

Kevin nodded. "I know," he said. "I think it's cool we're out there helping people, but I don't think Jesse would have wanted us moping around like martyrs." His eyes filled. "In fact, Jesse may have even given me the idea."

Izzy, Ava and Randy nodded—their eyes also misting over.

"Thanks Kev," Ava said sincerely.

"You're welcome," he said and looked directly at Randy—and winked.

"Whatever," Randy said, shaking his head. "I'm still going to get you."

Kevin slapped Randy's back proudly. "Actually, ladies," he said, "our friend Randy here said he was waiting for something big and just last night an opportunity presented itself..."

"What are you talking about?" Randy quickly interrupted. "I'm still waiting."

"Sure you are, Captain America," Izzy said, looking at Randy's arm. "So where did you get the scratches on your arm from?" she asked.

"Yeah, look at them," Ava said.

Randy shrugged. "I got into a fight with my land-lord's cat and lost."

"Yeah right," Ava countered.

Randy grinned. "No shame in it, though. Have you ever seen the size of that cat?"

Everyone laughed, while Kevin turned to Randy. "Nicely done, my friend. I'm just glad you're okay."

"I appreciate that," Randy said, "but I have no intention of going near that cat again."

"Well, if you ever need some hero support in the future, I'll be happy to help you put your cape on."

As they played cards, their laughter echoed down the street.

9

On Friday morning, a female college newspaper reporter approached Randy, notebook in hand. Randy kept walking.

"Randy Duhon, right?" she asked, in step with Randy.

"That's me," he said.

"By any chance, did you hear anything about an attempted sexual attack in the east parking lot last night?" she asked.

"No, I didn't," Randy said. "Did they get the guy?"

The reporter smiled. "Yes, they did. And according to the victim, some young hero appeared out of nowhere and saved her." She winked. "And I'm told that you look just like him."

"The sex offender?" Randy teased.

"No," she said, smirking. "The hero."

"I have a common face, I guess," Randy said, shrugging.

She snickered. "So you're not going to give me anything, huh?" she asked.

Randy stopped walking and faced the pretty reporter. "Actually, I am." He looked around the campus. "Look, everyone makes fun of the campus police.

They're an easy target. Truth is, though, they're under-staffed with a whole lot of area to cover. There's no way they can protect everyone on this campus and be everywhere at the same time." He shook his head. "I'd like to call a meeting for next Friday at noon to be held in the cafeteria. We need to start taking some respon-sibility for ourselves and I'm thinking that a student crime watch might be the right start. For a college with a Criminal Justice program, I'm hoping that we'll get some real support on this."

The young newspaper investigator wrote feverishly into her notebook. When she finally looked up, Randy asked, "Did you get all that?"

She nodded. "I did."

"Then that's your real story," he said. "Please run it."

"I will," she promised.

"Thanks," he said and as he started to walk away, he added, "Last night is old news. The question is, what are we going to do to prevent these attacks in the future?"

She nodded once and captured the final quote in her notebook.

~ ~ ~

On the girls' front porch—while the sky swelled with gray clouds, threatening an early snow—Ava was put-ting together baskets from the boxes of donated food items stacked in the corner. She was on her cell phone, talking as she worked. "Well, we're looking for non-per-ishable items." She listened and responded, "Yes, two other markets have already donated. I'm speaking with a newspaper reporter later this week and I'd really like to mention your market as well." While Ava listened, a smile spread across her face. "Thank you so much.

That's very generous! The food will be going to some very special people who have fed others their whole lives. It just makes sense that we provide them with a meal or two. I'll be by tomorrow afternoon to pick up your donations. Thanks again."

Ava hung up the cell phone and started assembling another food basket.

~ ~ ~

In the morning, as Ava walked through the college quad on her way to class, she answered her cell phone again. "Hello. Yes, I'm she. I'm following up on those three shut-ins that we spoke about earlier in the week." She listened. "Great. I'll email those addresses over to you this afternoon. When will the meal deliveries begin?" She listened again and smiled. "Wonderful, and does *daily* mean the weekends, as well?" She smiled wider. "Awesome! Thank you so much. We really appreciate it." Ava hung up, looked at her phone to check the time and picked up the pace to get to class.

~ ~ ~

Exhausted, Ava fought to stay awake during class. As she dozed off, Professor Larkin became insulted. "I'm sorry, Ms. Jacobs," he said, raising his voice with each word. "If we're keeping you awake, we can try to keep it down."

Ava's eyes flew open. "I'm...I'm sorry," she stammered.

"It must have been a lively party, huh?" Professor Larkin said. "A late one, right?"

"Not at all," she said.

"Okay, then tell us what has you napping during my class?" he said, sarcastically. "I doubt it's because of late-night studying."

Ava took a deep breath. "I needed to be there for a friend last night, that's all," she explained angrily. "But you have my undivided attention now, professor."

There were snickers from the other students in the room. After a long, harsh look from Professor Larkin, the class instruction resumed.

Ava yawned once and forced her eyes to stay open.

~ ~ ~

From the center of the college campus, Kevin and a small army of backpack-wearing cyclists started off on their long journey. It was an impressive sight—as they rode through the campus. Randy and Izzy were there to cheer on Kevin and his cavalry. The group then rode out the front gate until the last one disappeared.

~ ~ ~

That night on the front porch, Izzy, Ava and Randy still got together. Everyone was deep in thought. Finally, Izzy said, "I hope Kevin stays safe out there on the road."

"He said not to worry…it's only a long bike ride," Randy quipped.

"He told me the same thing," Ava added.

"That's so awesome," Izzy said, "what he's doing. Good for him."

Randy nodded. "That's our boy."

There was no poker that night. Instead, they sat together in silence.

~ ~ ~

On Friday afternoon, Randy stood before the crowd. There were several dozen students—most of them Criminal Justice majors—and a few faculty in attendance.

"I could go on and on today," Randy said, "trying to sell you on all the reasons for us to begin a student-run crime watch, but I'll make this simple." He referenced his notebook. "We've had three successful sexual attacks on campus in the past two years. And for one reason or another, there were two others that were unsuccessful." He looked up. "And we all know that there'll be more. I'm not saying we'll be able to stop every animal that steps foot on our campus, but I have no doubt that we'd be able to stop some of them." He paused. "So, for me it's real simple. If we can stop one of our own from becoming another statistic, from becoming a victim, then it's worth every second of our time and effort." Randy placed a blank book in front of him. "If you agree, I'd like you to sign your name under mine on this list today. We can work out the logistics later, but for now let's see what kind of force we can amass."

One student began clapping, who was followed by another— until everyone was applauding.

Randy watched in awe as a single line formed, with several dozen students waiting to sign up. He then looked over to see the college newspaper reporter writing into her notebook. He approached her. "Hey, I need a favor," he said.

"Oh, no worries," she said, "I planned on signing up and—"

"No, not that," he interrupted, "though that would be cool." He paused in thought. "No, the favor is... although I'd very much like you to run this story, with the hope of recruiting more crime watchers, I need you to keep my name out of it."

She was surprised. "Why?"

"Please," he repeated, "just don't use my name, okay?"

"Okay," she said, reluctantly.

Randy patted her on the shoulder before returning to the sign-ups.

~ ~ ~

Across town, Ava passed through the projects on her way to Mr. Dwyer's apartment. "Oh my God," she muttered and looked up. Although it hadn't even drizzled, a rainbow suddenly appeared—its vivid colors stacked one on top of the next. It was the type of sign that could not be denied. She nodded, thinking, *I'm exactly where I need to be.*

On the afternoon she'd first met Mr. Dwyer, she'd brought him a deep dish pizza and they played cribbage. There was nothing behind his eyes; just the distant gaze of a man waiting to die. But a few subsequent visits seemed to soften and even spark a fire back into his sapphire eyes.

~ ~ ~

Ava sat in Mr. Dwyer's kitchen, preparing a snack for the elderly man.

"Why do I need to leave the apartment, Ava?" Mr. Dwyer asked. "I have everything I need here."

"Sure," Ava teased, "everything but contact with other people."

"I have you," he said, smiling.

"Yes you do. And I'll keep coming over every chance I get." She paused. "When's the last time you left this apartment?"

The old man thought for a while, but couldn't remember.

"Just try it once," she prodded, smiling, "for me."

Mr. Dwyer grinned. "That's not fair. Why is it so important to you?"

"Because I know it'll increase the quality of your life." She nodded. "I've done the research. There's a poker game every Friday afternoon at the Council on Aging Hall. They'll send a bus to pick you up and drop you off, so there are no excuses there."

"I don't know," he said.

"Do you need me to teach you how to play poker?" she teased.

"I put two of my kids through college playing poker." He grinned. "You want to play me for your tuition money?"

"So a Friday game will be fun then, right?" she said.

The old man sighed heavily. "Okay, I'll try it," he said, finally surrendering.

Wearing her best smile, Ava nodded.

The two sat and watched TV together for a few minutes when Mr. Dwyer confessed, "Ava, from the first time you knocked on my door, I've honestly felt like God sent me a guardian angel." He matched her smile. "I hope you have one too."

Ava nodded. "I do," she said. "His name's Jesse."

~ ~ ~

Izzy and Ava were sitting together on the porch studying for finals, when a young couple—the woman pregnant—ascended their stairs.

"Excuse us for intruding, but is one of you Isabella Evans?" the man asked.

Izzy sat up, curious. "I am."

Without a word, the pregnant woman hurried to her and gave her a hug. Both Izzy and Ava were taken aback.

The man quickly explained. "Isabella, I'm Don and the woman hugging the life out of you right now is my wife, Tracy. Our four-year-old son, Cameron..." he became choked up, "...was dying from leukemia until you saved his life."

"She what?" Ava squealed.

While Tracy let go of Izzy, she turned to Ava. "Isabella was a perfect match for Cameron and donated her bone marrow. We didn't think..." Tracy began crying.

Don took over. "The radiation and chemotherapy treatments didn't work for Cameron. Three weeks ago, the doctors pretty much told us to say our good-byes to him." He paused to compose himself. "But an angel showed up out of nowhere and spared our boy's life." Don approached Izzy, who accepted his hug.

"So we came to say thank you," Tracy said, rubbing her belly, "and to ask your permission."

"Permission?" Izzy asked, confused.

"Tracy nodded. "We'd like to name our daughter, Isabella, if it's okay with you?"

"Oh, Iz," Ava cried.

Izzy was overwhelmed with emotion and could only nod.

The four sat together for a while, alternating between conversation and wiping away tears.

~ ~ ~

An hour later, as the sun set for the night, Izzy's surprise guests bid their farewell. She and Ava sat alone.

"Mono?" Ava snickered. "That was a good one."

"I'm sorry I lied to you," Izzy said, "I didn't like it."

"That's fine," Ava said and smiled. "Well, it looks like you just won four quarters," she teased.

Izzy looked hard at her friend. "No, Ava. Swear to me that you won't tell a soul."

"But why?"

"It just doesn't seem like it's something I should take credit for," Izzy explained. "It's bigger than that, you know?" She paused. "Besides, Jesse knows..."

"And so does God," Ava interrupted in a whisper.

"Exactly." Izzy smiled. "And that's my point, Ava. No one else has to know, okay?"

"Okay," Ava conceded.

~ ~ ~

Ten hours later, it was just past dusk when Kevin—covered in four days of sweat and dirt—led his exhausted troops through the college's front gate. While most of the bike riders could barely keep their eyes open, Kevin's emerald eyes sparkled with joy. "We did it!" he said aloud.

~ ~ ~

The sun rose in the east, chasing away the shadows on the campus quad. Izzy stood at a table, with other college-aged volunteers. A banner reading, ADULT LITERACY BOOK DRIVE hung across the front of the table. While college students and faculty stopped by to donate their used books, Izzy was on her cell phone with the local library. "I guess the bottom line is that you'll never have to throw away another book," she said. "We'll take them all. And we'll take care of storing them, moving them and distributing them. Can we meet next week to finalize the logistics?" She listened. "Fantastic! You just made my day."

~ ~ ~

That night, on Izzy and Ava's front porch, the crew gathered for their weekly get-together and to celebrate their recent achievements with a pizza party.

"One more week to go until Christmas," Ava said, "until we see who won the contest."

"Everyone ready?" Izzy asked.

The boys nodded but remained quiet.

"Silence until the end," Ava said. "I love it."

IO

The college cafeteria was decorated for the holidays, everything covered in red and green. Kevin stood tall at a podium in the middle of the dining room, addressing a small audience of scholarship sponsors and supporters. "Not long ago," he began, "I was inspired by the generous spirit of my late friend, Jesse Cabral, to make a positive difference in this world. As a poor kid who has struggled to fund my own way through college, I decided that I wanted to establish a scholarship... enough money for some kid to go to school. Not a hand out, but *a hand up*." He took a deep breath and nodded before continuing, "...with the expectation that each recipient will pay it forward when they are in the position to do so." He looked up from the podium and scanned the smiling crowd before him. "The support I received was overwhelming and my dream of creating one scholarship ended up becoming two, with enough annual pledges for two scholarships each year going forward."

Applause echoed through the room.

Kevin continued. "I can also see the potential for this one inspired idea to keep growing and increasing until we can help lots of kids get into college...good students that may not have had the opportunity otherwise."

The applause grew louder.

"I'll be spending much of my free time during the spring semester reviewing applications for the first two *Hand Up Scholarships*," Kevin said, wearing the biggest smile. "And I can't imagine anything that would make me happier."

The applause reached a spine-tingling volume. Kevin fought back his emotions. He was overjoyed.

After enjoying a potluck dinner, everyone prepared to leave. Professor Wishart, a respected faculty member, approached Kevin. "People are going to remember your name around here, Kevin Robinson," he said with a wink.

"Nope. I'm just the messenger," Kevin said. "It's the name Jesse that people need to remember."

The wise man nodded. As he turned to walk away, he stopped. "Just make sure you select recipients who are worthy of this extraordinary gift," he said.

"I will," Kevin promised, "because we need this to spread like some inspired wildfire."

~ ~ ~

Ava finished the final edit on her human interest piece, *Life on the River*, and wondered how Mrs. LeComte would react to her story being told. She'd spent ten times the effort on that one piece than any college reporter would have ever bothered. But it was a one-shot deal for both her and Mrs. LeComte. *I need to get it right*, Ava decided. Even Izzy pretended to complain about all the time Ava spent on the computer.

~ ~ ~

Ava finally turned it in. The editor called two days later. "Not a bad piece for your first," he said. "I had to make the usual changes though."

"Thanks," Ava told him.

There was a pause. "Listen, if you're looking to write some more, I have plenty of work that I need to assign," he offered.

"Thanks," Ava told him, "I'll have to check my schedule to see what I can fit." It was the best way she knew of saying she had no further interest.

"Fair enough. Just let me know," he said before there was a dial tone.

~ ~ ~

It was a random Tuesday morning when Ava picked up a copy of the college newspaper, *The Fighting Eagle*, and flipped through it. Her spirit soared. The piece was buried on page seven, but its placement didn't matter. She grabbed ten copies and raced off to the Rolling Hills Retirement Home to share it with Mrs. LeComte.

~ ~ ~

Ava sat on the edge of the old woman's bed and took a deep breath. "Life on the River," Ava read and was surprised when her eyes started to swell with tears.

Mrs. LeComte grabbed Ava's hand and nodded for her to continue.

"On the twelfth of May, a baby girl was born to proud parents in Fall River, Massachusetts. Little did they know—Marie LeComte's life would be an amazing one..."

Mrs. LeComte began to cry. "Oh sweetheart," she whimpered and squeezed Ava's hand.

Ava studied the woman's face for a moment. "Should I continue, Mrs. LeComte?"

"Oh yes...please do," the woman said before closing her eyes—to bask in the details of her existence on earth.

~ ~ ~

A week before Christmas, Professor McKee happened by the front porch and asked, "So none of you are going home for the Christmas break?"

Kevin, Ava, Randy and Izzy all shook their heads. "We're staying here," Randy announced.

"With Jesse," Ava added.

The teacher smiled. "That's what I figured," she said and walked away.

~ ~ ~

Each of them wrote home, letting their families know that they were going to spend this last Christmas at college together. In lieu of gifts, they requested decorations and food.

Izzy's dad surprised them by bringing up a real blue spruce pine tree; he left it in the tree stand on the porch with a note: *Merry Christmas, guys. As you share the spirit of the holidays together, let it heal you.*

Ava's parents sent a supermarket gift card for two hundred dollars with a note: *For food only, please.*

"We will, Mom," Ava announced aloud and laughed. "We'll use whatever cash we have for beer and wine."

Kevin's family sent a care package with enough sweets—minus the fruitcake—to cause the early onset of diabetes.

Professor McKee also left a box of canned food on the porch. The note read, *Consider it a small visit from karma.*

Randy's parents shipped a huge box of old Christmas decorations to the boys' apartment. When Randy lugged it over to the front porch, all four of them sifted through its contents. "Looks like someone saved a trip to the landfill," Kevin teased.

Randy nodded. "To you, maybe," he said, "but my entire childhood is in this box." He began pulling out one item after the next and his eyes were set on fire. "Every Christmas since I was a baby..." he mumbled.

The rest of them shared some discreet smirks, while allowing Randy his moment of nostalgia.

From tangled strands of lights that intermittently worked to crocheted red and green afghans that smelled like moth balls, there was a little bit of everything in the massive box. A huge plastic poster of Santa Claus was attached to the back of a creased cardboard fireplace, which probably looked pretty nice the first fifteen years it was used. But that was at least ten years ago. A box within the box revealed faded and chipped ornaments. Several unused boxes of tinsel lay at the bottom, along with a porcelain Christmas tree—illuminated by multi-colored lights. Kevin became excited when he saw it; he yanked it out of the box and hurried to plug it in. "It works," he said.

"And it's ugly," Ava said.

"It sure is," he admitted, "but it's also rare."

"What?" Randy asked.

Kevin nodded. "I've seen them online and they're worth money now." He looked at Randy. "Unless you're attached to it, we could—"

"—put it on eBay," Randy finished for his friend. "It obviously means more to me than my parents." He grinned. "And the beer means more to me than the porcelain tree."

Everyone laughed, while Izzy and Ava positioned the twinkling ceramic tree for a photo to place on eBay.

Staying up late into the night, they transformed Izzy and Ava's apartment into a magical—although poor—wonderland.

~ ~ ~

On Christmas Eve, as the snow began to fall, all four friends passed beneath a deformed, plastic ball of mistletoe to gather together on the porch. The girls claimed the glider, while the boys dragged their chairs against the apartment's faded clapboard, where they could bury themselves under the same blankets they usually made fun of. With the window open, it was Randy's turn to have his cell phone's play list plugged in. He chose to remain on memory lane with a play list that included Nat King Cole, Dean Martin, Elvis Presley and every other artist that his parents forced him to listen to as a boy—but whom he'd since missed.

At one point, Ava slapped the iPod, shutting it off. For a long while, the four sat together in silence—listening to the frozen wind caroling through the icicle-draped trees. The white ground blended beautifully with the gray sky, broken only by the soft light being emitted from windows up and down both sides of the desolate street as families celebrated in their own ways and traditions.

In the silence, Kevin whispered, "I really miss Jesse."

"Me too," Ava said, her voice choked with emotion.

As though he were going to speak, Randy took a deep breath. But he only exhaled, his feelings betrayed in a wounded sigh.

Izzy shook her head. "But he's with us," she whispered, tears glistening in her eyes. "Can't you feel him?"

Ava grabbed her friend's arm and held on tight. "I do," she said. "I really do."

"Me too," Kevin said.

Randy nodded. "But not just here," he said. "Not just now." He took another deep breath, trying to compose himself. "I feel Jesse with me in everything I do."

"Me too," Kevin repeated. "And this may sound crazy, but I'm always asking myself *what would Jesse think* before I do pretty much anything."

Through her sniffles, Izzy laughed. "That's not a bad compass to use," she whimpered.

"I know," Kevin agreed. "I feel blessed to have him with me."

"Me too," they said in chorus.

For a moment, they sat in silence together—until Ava whispered, "Merry Christmas, Jesse"—as though he were sitting right there beside them.

One by one, the other three echoed the same.

And in response, the icy wind sang through the frozen pines.

~ ~ ~

When they finally sat to eat, the girls ensured that a place was set for Jesse at the head of their humble table. No one even considered claiming the seat.

II

The following night, in the bitter cold, the four friends bundled up and returned to the front porch. It seemed appropriate to present the tally of deeds to Professor McKee, their only witness and judge.

"When we graduate in the spring, I've heard that the college is honoring Jesse with a Bachelor's degree," Izzy said.

"Well, it's only right," McKee said, nodding. "Though they won't be honoring him nearly as much as you guys have."

Kevin cleared his throat. "This may sound strange, but this contest to honor Jesse's memory has become just as important to me as graduating in the spring."

"That doesn't sound strange at all," McKee said. "In a way, you'll all be graduating twice."

They awaited an explanation.

"In the spring, you'll all be graduating from higher education," she said, "but tonight...tonight, you're graduating from childhood into an adult life of caring and compassion." She took a deep breath and sighed. "I spend hours filling your heads, trying to prepare you for that big bad world out there. But as I think about it, I've only told my own children three things:

have the courage to be who God made you to be; take responsibility for your life—whether it's happiness or misery, it's your choice; and if you work hard enough and never lose faith, dreams really do come true." She smiled. "And I've watched each one of you do exactly that for weeks now."

"We've definitely tried our best," Randy said proudly.

Professor McKee shook her head. "No, you've done more than *try*, Randy," she said and then searched each of their eyes. "You guys went out into the world and did it! You took action, real positive action, and there are already many lives that will never be the same again because of it."

The four friends couldn't wipe the smiles from their faces.

"So let's hear it," McKee said. "Let's hear about all the amazing things Jesse inspired you to do."

Izzy stepped forward first. "Well, I ran a book drive for four weeks to raise money and collect books for adult literacy."

Ava cleared her throat to report more, but Izzy quickly gave her the evil eye and a subtle shake of the head. The others picked up on it, but never questioned it. Professor McKee grinned. Ava's eyes filled with proud tears for her friend, while she kept their secret.

"All together," Izzy said, "I raised thirty two hundred dollars, more boxes of books than I can count and a local library connection that should generate free books for years to come. More importantly, I raised tons of awareness and even recruited a few serious volunteers who will be getting involved."

"So you've already gathered a following," McKee noted. "Good for you, Izzy. Jesse would be proud."

Izzy nodded and the first tears streamed down her cheeks. "I can't even begin to explain everything I've learned over the past few weeks, but it's amazing to me how fortunate…" she paused, "…and guilty I feel for having everything I have."

The rest of them agreed.

As though they were in class, Professor McKee turned to the others. "Randy, I think we all know that you were responsible for saving one of our freshmen from a brutal sexual attack."

Randy smiled coyly. "I have no idea what you're talking about," he said, "though I did hear that some known rapist was stopped before he could take another victim." He grinned wider. "The police think it's enough to put him away for a long time."

"That's our Crime Fighter," Kevin teased.

"You mean our Super Hero?" Ava corrected him.

While they all laughed, Professor McKee stared at Randy. "Good for you," she said.

Randy shook his head. "I guess I want to help people because there was a time in my life when I was bullied." He pointed to Kevin. "After Kevin's gorilla stunt, I realized that the campus police are incredibly understaffed and that we have a responsibility to look after ourselves." He shrugged. "Protect our own, you know?"

They all nodded.

"So I've spent the last few weeks establishing a campus crime watch that will be run by students next year," he added. "Hopefully, it'll be in place for years to come."

The wise professor nodded. "Goodness," she said. "To think of all the people you may be saving from becoming victims."

While Randy blushed, Kevin proudly added, "Not bad for a communications major."

Randy chuckled. "And therein lies the challenge. I've already decided to take Criminal Justice courses next year so I can graduate with two majors."

"You what?" Izzy asked, shocked. "You're staying for a fifth year?"

Randy smiled. "I am."

"No radio internship?" Kevin teased.

Randy laughed. "I'm not sure what I'll do when I graduate...maybe join the campus police, military service, or even municipal law enforcement. Whatever it is, thanks to Jesse I know I'll be serving a purpose much bigger than just myself from here on."

"Incredible," Professor McKee sighed and then turned to Ava. "And you, Ava?"

"I've been volunteering with the elderly," Ava said nervously. "Though it's not as important as what Randy's done."

"I'm sure it is to them," Professor McKee interrupted.

Ava smiled proudly. "This may sound weird, but it's not about anything I've done or am doing. In fact, I don't have to do anything. I just need to be with them, so they know they're not alone in this world and that another human being cares." She looked at Professor McKee, her eyes filled with gratitude. "It may not mean a lot to most people, but Professor McKee's right; it means everything to each of them and that makes it worth every second I spend."

In that moment, McKee became teary-eyed. "Brilliant!" she said. "I can't tell you how proud I am right now." She took a deep breath to retain her composure. "And how proud Jesse must be, looking down on you guys right now."

"He'd better be," Izzy joked.

All four laughed—wiping away more happy tears.

Without waiting to be called, Kevin stepped forward. "As my friends know, I've pretty much had to beg, borrow and almost steal to pay for college." He shook his sorrowful head. "I realized when I was very young that without a secondary education, I'd never get the opportunities needed to climb out of poverty and create a better future for myself and my children, if I ever have any." He took a deep breath and turned to face Professor McKee directly. "I was raised by my grandparents, who created miracles by keeping food on the table and a roof over our heads. I always felt ashamed that we had nothing, but the older I got the more I realized that life was all about creating our own circumstances." He shook his head. "The same people who look down on kids from the ghetto could never even dream of ways of getting out themselves...especially at eighteen years old."

"So what kind of miracle were you inspired to perform over the past few weeks?" Professor McKee asked.

"All I did was ride my bike from Boston to the tip of the Cape," Kevin replied.

"Is that all?" Randy teased.

Kevin smiled. "And with some very generous sponsors, I've been able to create some awareness of the problem, as well as two annual college scholarships for impoverished, inner-city kids—" He got choked up and needed to stop for a moment. "—so that they'll also have a shot at college and a decent life." As soon as Kevin finished, he was overcome with emotion and began to cry.

His friends joined him and they all began to sob. With incredible love and respect, Professor McKee quietly looked on.

"I don't mean to get all emotional on everyone," Kevin managed between sobs, "but it's just that I'm so grateful to Jesse for—"

"—for the greatest gift anyone can receive," the teacher interrupted, "...a purpose."

The four friends were in awe at the miracles taking place in their lives. The emotions were overwhelming.

"So how do you pick a winner," McKee asked, "when each of your deeds has been hugely impacting to the people whom you've touched?"

They each shrugged.

She searched each of their faces. "So that's it then?" she asked. "The contest is over?"

"Nope," Randy said, sniffling. "As far as I'm concerned, it's just gotten started."

They all nodded in agreement.

"I was thinking the same thing," Izzy said. "The way I see it, it'll take a *hundred* Christmases to bring Jesse's memory the honor it deserves and—"

"—and carry on his torch of kindness," Kevin added, nodding. "Yup, a lifetime wouldn't be long enough."

Ava smiled at her friends. "But four lifetimes might," she whispered.

They all smiled.

"It seems to me that you've all won," Professor McKee said.

Ava grabbed the glass jar containing the four quarters. "But we still need to decide who walks away with the winnings," she said.

While Izzy wrapped her arms around Ava's shoulder, Professor McKee spent a moment in thought. She winked at Ava. "Since any one of you could take the pot, why don't you just flip for it?"

They each grabbed a quarter.

Kevin announced, "On three, we all flip. Heads side-up stays in." He smiled. "One, two, three…"

They all flipped. Kevin and Ava were out in the first round.

Izzy and Randy flipped again. As their coins settled, Randy yelled, "No!"

"Sorry, Rockin' Randy," Kevin teased.

Smiling, Randy picked up the quarters and handed them to Izzy. Ava smiled at the irony.

Izzy held the four coins for a moment before sliding them into her pocket. Hugs were then exchanged all around, with Professor McKee joining in. "Congratulations," she said, "and Merry Christmas."

~ ~ ~

Izzy was walking down the sidewalk, talking on her cell phone. "I don't know what Randy's planning, Ava," she said. "All I know is that he's been dying to even the score with Kevin ever since that radio station prank and I don't want to miss it." She listened and laughed. "Okay, I'll see you there."

Two blocks later, she approached one of Kevin's new friends—a homeless man. She reached into her pocket and pulled out the four quarters. Looking around to ensure no one was watching, she dropped the money into the man's paper cup.

"God bless you," the poor soul whispered.

"No," Izzy said, shaking her head. "God bless Jesse."

A Christmas Wish

Mama's cottage shimmered in a festive glow, a mix of colored lights and lots of tinsel. The last of the raviolis were long gone and Nat King Cole had just finished singing "O Come All Ye Faithful" when the family grabbed their coats, said their goodbyes and headed out the door.

Mama stopped Joan. "Let Brian stay the night. Your Uncle Sal's offered to drive us into Little Italy to do some Christmas shopping tomorrow. We've been talking about it for weeks and he's excited."

Joan smiled. "That sounds great, Ma. At least you won't have to take the train in this year."

"True," the old lady said, grinning, "but knowing your Uncle Sal, it'll cost me twice as much in gas money."

Joan laughed.

Mama laughed right along with her, never letting on about the excruciating pain that throbbed in her legs.

"Okay," Joan said, pulling Brian in for a long hug. "Just call me when you get sick of him and I'll be by to get him," she teased.

Brian picked up on the joke and squeezed his mother tight.

"Then you'll never see him again," Mama said, stealing him away for herself.

Just then, Mama's granddaughter Steph stepped into the kitchen; she was holding her jacket, not wearing it. Sensing that something was wrong, Mama quickly bid farewell to Joan and turned to Steph. "How 'bout you stay a while and help me clean up?" She shook her head and lifted her curled, arthritic hands. "These hands aren't good for anything anymore."

With a suspicious grin, Steph threw her coat over the kitchen chair and rolled up her sleeves. "What first?" she asked.

"Why don't you start with the dishes while I put Brian to bed," Mama said. "We have a big day tomorrow and he needs his beauty sleep."

Without complaint, Brian hugged his cousin and said, "Nigh nigh." Mama then escorted him off to the bathroom to make him brush his teeth.

Since the doctors had predicted—sixteen years before—that Brian would never walk or talk or develop normally, the vast majority of Mama's time and effort, her life's purpose, was spent in the relentless pursuit of instilling independence in her grandson and ensuring that his doctors were wrong. Yet there were times when one of her other grandchildren needed her undivided attention. This was definitely one of those times.

~ ~ ~

Steph had no sooner finished washing the first pan when she felt the family matriarch standing beside her at the sink.

"You sure you can't tag along with me and Brian on our Christmas stroll tomorrow?" Mama asked.

"I wish I could, Mama. I do. But this has been a tough semester and I have a pile of schoolwork that…"

"Say no more," the old woman interrupted. "School comes first!"

While they talked about college life and grades, Steph watched as her clever grandmother's hands put out three times the amount of work that she could. After drying the last plate and putting it away in the cupboard, Mama slung the dishcloth over her shoulder, peered into her granddaughter's eyes and asked, "So what do you want for Christmas this year?"

On appearance, this was a simple enough question—but they both knew that it was so much more. In reality, it was an opportunity for Steph to open up and bare her soul.

Without ever asking them, Steph's legs carried her to Mama's kitchen table where she sat down and prepared for her confession. Again, her insightful grandmother was right there beside her. "The courage to be true to myself," Steph finally answered, "…once and for all." Months before, she had let her grandmother know that she was gay. And although Mama had never even blinked at the testimony, Steph was still having a difficult time with it.

Mama smiled and placed her hand on Steph's hands—where it stayed. "Well, that might just be the best Christmas gift you ever receive."

"If I ever do receive it," Steph said.

Mama squeezed her granddaughter's hands with surprising strength. "Sweetheart, that's a gift that only you can give to yourself. We've talked about this. You're perfect…exactly the way God made you." She smiled. "Have you been a good girl this year?" she teased.

Steph snickered. "I wish it were that easy, Mama."

"Being easy or difficult shouldn't even factor in. Your cousin Brian should have taught you that by now." Mama searched Steph's eyes. "And why wouldn't it be easy?"

Steph shook her head, while her eyes filled. "Because..."

"Because it's about having faith," Mama interrupted, "and taking that first step when you can't see anything in front of you to step on, right?"

Steph nodded, trying desperately to internalize the wise woman's words.

"When you kids were young, I taught each one of you how to make a Christmas wish come true. Do you remember?"

"I do," Steph said, smiling at the beloved memory. "You said that all we had to do was close our eyes, picture the wish that we want to come true, and then open our eyes to seal it with a wink."

"That's right!" Mama said. "You remember." She studied her granddaughter's eyes. "Well then, what are you waiting for?"

Steph began to laugh until she realized that her grandmother was serious. With a nod, she closed her eyes, painted some very vivid pictures in her mind, and then opened her eyes—to seal the wish with a wink.

Mama smiled wide and returned the wink. "It's sealed then! Now all you have to do is wait for your Christmas wish to come true."

Steph took a deep breath, surprised that she believed the tiny woman as much today as she did when she was a little girl.

"So could you really picture it?" Mama asked, grinning.

Steph nodded. Her mind immediately returned to that fateful night where the wish had begun, and she shared each glorious detail with her grandmother.

~ ~ ~

Though she'd refused again and again, Steph finally allowed herself to be talked into going on a blind date. "But if it doesn't work, then it's the last time," she vowed.

Melissa was a petite beauty with dark hair and green eyes that sparkled when Steph met her at her front door. From the first impression, Steph figured, *This entire night's going to be a waste of time.*

The Elephant & Castle, an English-style pub located in downtown Boston, had a row of red and green stained-glass windows just above a horseshoe-shaped bar. Walls of rich mahogany panels climbed up to a forest green ceiling crafted of tin. Hints of the UK and India were everywhere, each trinket and picture a trophy of some far off adventure or exotic exploration. Frosted wall lamps, accented in brass, lit the place in a soothing and serene light. Plaques of family crests from the old country, along with shelves of books, created a living room atmosphere. *It feels like we're in a British lodge, taking a break from the fox hunt,* Steph thought.

The hostess escorted Steph and her date to a small table off in the corner. *There'll be no chance of quiet conversation,* Steph knew. Pints of dark, bitter ale made the bar crowd talk in a chorus that could have been mistaken for cheering at a Manchester United football game.

"Nice place," Steph commented.

Melissa shrugged. She was clearly unimpressed.

Steph shook her head and dove into a menu that featured kidney pie, bangers and beans, and fish and chips wrapped in newspaper. *The fish and chips*, she decided right away and then began small talk with Melissa until the food arrived.

The Lion King had been playing in Beantown for three months straight and Steph had been lucky to score a pair of tickets for one of its final performances. Newly restored, the Opera House was recently returned to its pristine condition of yesteryear. Beyond an intricately detailed, wrought iron entrance, Steph gestured for Melissa to enter before her. The wide lobby was lined with full-length mirrors, a tiny ticket office and posters that advertised several upcoming productions. Past the lobby, a foyer of ornate marble and nostalgic red velvet wallpaper opened up to two giant, winding staircases off to each side, both leading directly to the mezzanine level. Ballroom chandeliers of crystal illuminated the growing crowd. As she took it all in, Steph felt her mouth widen. She looked over at Melissa. As expected, Melissa was in her own world; someplace far away from where they now stood.

Minutes before being seated, Steph spotted an intriguing beauty standing alone in a corner. The woman was her age, with dark, flowing hair and a pair of shining eyes to match. Her rich olive complexion betrayed subtle hints of Mediterranean blood. She was well built and Steph couldn't help but study her body language. She wasn't hard to decipher: she was confident, single and all woman. One question remained, though: *Is she gay?*

As a slow stampede moved toward the theater doors, the lovely stranger's friend took her place beside her. They looked very much alike. *A family resemblance,*

Steph thought, and sighed. *And she's not here with a guy.* Steph glanced over at Melissa who was studying her ticket, and then looked back at the stranger. *What a wasted opportunity,* she thought.

Just then, the mystery lady looked straight at Steph—right into to her eyes—and smiled.

The brief exchange took her breath away. As the crowd closed in all around them, she couldn't help herself and returned the smile. A moment later, Melissa stepped beside Steph and grabbed her arm.

The stranger offered a pouty grin and then shrugged, playfully.

Steph rolled her eyes, turning the stranger's grin into a devilish smirk. Steph felt her knees weaken.

The doors to the theater opened, revealing a vast space of grandeur and architectural glory. A vaulted ceiling that touched the heavens revealed a powder blue painting of winged cherubs at play. Tight rows of seats pitched downward toward a massive stage, while a drawn, crimson curtain waited to be parted for a night of certain magic.

For eighty dollars per seat, Steph and Melissa were five rows back from the conductor's bobbing head. In awe, Steph took her seat and surveyed the room. The details were magnificent.

As the house lights went down and the orchestra struck its first note, Steph scanned the crowd one last time and spotted her. The mysterious stranger was seated to her left, a few rows back. And she was smiling at her.

Though *The Lion King* was a spiritually uplifting production, Steph felt a film of coldness, an awkwardness between herself and Melissa. *First date...and last,* she assured herself.

Melissa glanced over at her and half-smiled.

She must be thinking the same thing, Steph thought.

At the start of the chaotic intermission, Steph turned to Melissa. "Can I get you a drink?"

"White wine, please."

Braving the long line, Steph finally stepped up to the small cash bar and ordered, "One white wine and one diet cola, please."

As the barmaid pushed Steph's change toward her and hurried to take the next order, Steph turned to find the mystery lady standing directly behind her. "Oh, hi," Steph blurted.

"Hi," she said with a smile and quickly placed her order at the bar. "Two red wines." She then turned to Steph, her eyebrows raised. "Enjoying the show?"

Steph was thrilled with the opportunity to explain her painful dilemma. "Just the typical blind date to remind me of why I never agree to go on blind dates."

While juggling her change and two plastic cups of red wine, the woman chuckled. "I hate them, too." As though they weren't actual strangers, there was a comfortable pause. "Well, good luck," she finally said and returned to her friend who'd been watching closely.

Steph inhaled deeply. The stranger's perfume was intoxicating.

Just as the house lights flickered to announce that the show was about to get underway, Steph caught the woman's gaze once again and swallowed hard. *She's gorgeous.*

The second act was no less awkward with Melissa than the first. Steph tried to will Simba and Nala's heartwarming tale toward a speedier conclusion.

As they followed the slothful mass out of the theater, Steph saw the woman she'd been fantasizing about all night. She was standing off to the side again. This time, it was as if she was waiting for something— or someone.

"I have to use the ladies room," Melissa muttered. "I'll only be a minute."

Steph smiled. "No problem. I see an old friend I'd like to say hi to. How 'bout I meet you at the bar when you're through?"

She nodded and quickly scanned the crowd for Steph's "old friend." The search was brief. Mother Nature was calling loud and clear.

Steph approached her infatuation. "Hi," she said, sheepishly.

"Hi."

"I know this is going to seem terrible—because I'm supposed to be on a date right now—but I figured that if I didn't ask you now, I may never see you again and I didn't want to take the chance that we would never..."

The woman stopped Steph by placing a small, white business card into her hand. "I know. Call me."

Steph looked down at it.

"I'm Lauren," she said, breaking the silence between them. "And this is my sister Ana."

She shook both their hands. "I'm Steph."

Just then, Melissa returned. Not knowing what else to do, Steph introduced them. "Melissa, this is my friend Lauren."

The girls shook hands. Grinning at the bizarre situation, Ana shook her head.

Lauren turned to Steph. "Nice to see you again," she said, "Goodnight."

As Steph escorted Melissa out of the building, Melissa turned to her. "How long did you say you knew Lauren?" she asked.

Steph shrugged. "A little while."

~ ~ ~

Steph emerged from her story to see her grandmother wearing the same smile that she now wore.

"And how long ago was this chance meeting?" Mama asked.

"Two weeks ago...tonight."

"So when do you and Lauren plan to go out?" she asked with a smile.

"I have theater tickets for tomorrow night, but..."

"But?"

"But I sense that there may be no turning back for me after Lauren."

Mama rose from her chair. "You don't need courage, sweetheart. What you need is to realize that there's no turning back from who you are...from what's in your heart." She approached Steph, kissed her forehead and said, "I'll expect your call tomorrow night, and I don't care how late it is." With a yawn, she was off to bed.

Steph sat at the kitchen table in the silence for a long while. *Maybe it's best if there is nothing to step onto,* she thought. *Maybe it's best if I finally just let myself fall.*

~ ~ ~

The following afternoon, Uncle Sal circled the block four times before he found a parking spot at the end of Hanover Street. Mama eased out of the car and spent a few moments on the sidewalk stretching out her throbbing legs. Brian jumped out of the car and, seeming to sense her physical pain, he began to massage her back. Finally prepared to start down memory lane, she watched as Uncle Sal played with the radio knob, searching for Christmas music. She opened the passenger side door. "Aren't you coming with us?" she asked, confused.

He shook his head. "Are you crazy? Finding this parking spot was like hitting the lottery. It won't happen twice."

"But the parking spot is yours now, Sal."

He shook his head again.

"So you're going to just sit here for the whole day?" she asked, realizing that he had no intentions of joining them.

He nodded. "Yup, and I'll be fine. Just bring me something to eat when you guys come back."

She looked down the long street. "That might be a while, Sal," she admitted.

"No need to rush. I ate a big breakfast." He finally found the right station and smiled as he listened to Elvis crooning about having a blue Christmas. With one last nod, he eased back into his leather seat and got comfortable. "Go have fun...and take your time. I'll be here when you get back."

Mama shook her head and looked at Brian. He returned the headshake to her. Before she closed the car door, she said, "I'll grab you a veal parm sandwich from Rosa's on the way back."

Uncle Sal's smile grew wider. "Perfect," he said. "Extra sauce, please...oh, and don't tell her I'm here."

Mama laughed. "I think she's probably over you by now, Romeo," she said, and shut the car door.

Though his voice was muffled, Mama heard him say, "You'd be surprised." With a chuckle, she and Brian walked away.

No more than half-block up Hanover Street, Mama stopped in her tracks. She looked up and waited. Steel gray clouds were hovering, turning the world dark. The heavy scent of dampness clung to the ground, while the air was brisk and clean, biting at the lungs. In that moment, in the silence, every living creature seemed to pause and wait. As if it were a miracle sent from above, in the faintest light, a glittering speck tumbled to the earth—followed by another. Not a moment later, thousands of tiny rhinestones spiraled downward, dancing in the wind like innocent, playful toddlers. The silence was broken by Brian's laughter and Mama's chest warmed with love at the sound of it. The dreadful horizon was suddenly painted a soft pastel pink, as the earth's crust was frosted wedding cake white. Growing in numbers and velocity, the snowflakes fell and began to conceal the wear and tear of all that they touched. Within minutes, the world was transformed, renewed, while the joy in Brian's laughter echoed down the street.

"God is good," Mama told him, grateful for the miracle of another new beginning.

Brian nodded. "God god," he agreed.

Hand in hand, they continued on their journey.

Christmas lights, strung from pole-to-pole, struggled to twinkle beyond the gathering snow. The smells of garlic and aged cheese filled the air, broken by the occasional scent of burnt caramel. "I really do love Christmas," Mama confessed aloud, as she peeked into each brownstone they passed.

"Yets," Brian agreed, mimicking the woman's every move. "Ho...Ho...Ho!"

Mama stopped and turned to him. "After all these years, you still think that Christmas is about Santa Claus?"

He nodded. "Ho...Ho...Ho!"

She laughed. "You're such a stinker!"

He threw his arm around her and they shuffled on through a blanket of white.

As they strolled along, Mama rambled on about the old neighborhood to her attentive audience. "Years ago, even on a pauper's pay, we all wore our best on Sundays and no one missed church. We weren't holiday Catholics back then, but people very committed to our faith. The neighborhood priest, Father Fazzina, was considered royalty when I was a kid. In payment for his discreet forgiveness of our sins, we nearly genuflected every time we saw him.

"And everyone talked with their hands. My pa used to say, 'If we put our hands in our pockets, we'd have nothing to say.'" She shrugged. "Phrases like 'on my mother's soul' and 'not for nothing' were as common as old women blessing themselves a hundred times a day."

She looked at Brian. He was still nodding, doing his best to follow along.

"Everything the neighborhood did was hard," she continued. "We worked hard, loved hard, and played hard. I always wondered, though, why everyone spoke of life being better in Italy. In a million years, not one of them would have ever given up their American citizenship, packed up and returned, surrendering the freedoms that they enjoyed here. Instead, we enjoyed the best of both worlds by creating a little bit of the old country right in the neighborhood.

"We called this place Little Italy because it was just that. Shops sold everything from crystal stemware to expensive espresso machines made of handbanged copper. And anything imported from the old country was valued more than anything produced here—whether it was better or not." She laughed at the thought of it and shook her head.

Their first stop was the butcher shop. As Brian opened the door for his hobbling grandmother, the brass bell rang. The butcher immediately appeared from the back room, his crimson-stained coat looking a bit tighter on him than it had during their last visit. *Someone had a prosperous year,* Mama decided.

His eyes lit up when he saw the pair. "I was wondering when you two would show up," he said, offering a gap-toothed smile.

"Hello Vincent," Mama greeted him before surveying the chalk specials board above his head. "What's your best deal?" she asked.

"I'd say the birds were fed much better than the pigs this year, Angela," he reported.

"Great. I'll take the two biggest turkeys you have."

With a nod, the man disappeared into the back room. Mama turned to Brian. "But you're going to have to carry them this year, Brian, okay? Mama's legs won't hold out."

"K," he said, and curled his arm to show off his bicep.

Mama gave it a squeeze. "What a big, strong man you are now," she said, adding a whistle for effect.

He giggled in delight. When the butcher returned with the two massive birds, Brian was more than happy to take them off his hands. Mama knew that, if he had to, he would have carried ten of them—without complaint.

After collecting her change, Mama watched as her grandson strutted proudly toward the door. *And to think that the doctors said he would never walk,* she thought. *Stupid doctors!*

"All the best," Vincent called out to the two of them, as they reached the door.

"And the same to you," Mama told him. "Have a Merry Christmas."

Brian waved. "Bye Bence."

One block later, in the bitter air, Mama pressed on the rectory buzzer—even after the young priest appeared in the threshold. As the pious man made his way across the frosted courtyard, he fumbled to put on his jacket. Mama watched on, amused. He unlatched the wrought iron gate. "Hello, Mrs. DiMartino," he said, still buttoning his wool coat.

"Hello, Father." She studied both turkeys before instructing Brian to hand over the bigger of the two. "This is for the family who needs it most this Christmas...in my mother's memory."

"Oh, how wonderful," he said, bobbling the heavy bird in his arms. "The Perry family has fallen on some hard times and..."

Mama threw up her hand to stop him. "I don't need to know where it's going, Father." She locked eyes with him. "And I wish to remain anonymous, as well... okay?"

He nodded. "Of course," he said, struggling against the cold and the weight of the turkey. "My apologies."

"No worries," Mama said. "We both know that if I get credit for it here, then I don't get to claim it later... when I'm trying to negotiate my way past those pearly gates."

He smiled. "I'm pretty sure that you won't have a problem there, Mrs. DiMartino."

She returned his smile, and added a wink. "Thanks," she said, "I'll tell Saint Peter you said so."

He laughed, nodded his appreciation one last time and then scurried back toward rectory with the massive turkey.

The next stop was at The Mall, an abandoned court-yard where the statue of the Virgin Mother awaited them. Mama grabbed Brian's hand and went very slowly to her knees. Once she was safely into prayer position, Brian joined her on the snow-covered con-crete.

Five minutes later, Mama tapped his shoulder. He stood and helped her to her feet. This time, it took both his hands. After catching her breath, she told Brian, "I prayed that your brother will come home soon from the war." She looked skyward. "Safe and sound, Lord," she prayed aloud.

Brian sighed. "Low Rin."

"I love Ross, too," she said. "And it's a very honor-able thing that he's doing over there...but I won't be able to sleep right until he's finally home." She grabbed the crucifix that hung around her neck and kissed it.

Locking her arm into Brian's, they walked away—with Brian muttering his own plea to God.

After a little more shopping and a whole lot of gawk-ing, Mama and Brian finally made their way to Lucia's at the end of Hanover Street. Mama's eyes immedi-ately became distant, as she spent some time with her memories of the past. Her glowing smile revealed that they were cherished.

"Ate Mama," Brian finally announced, breaking the silence.

Her head flew up and her eyes returned to the pres-ent. "You're hungry, sweetheart?" she asked, her own stomach rumbling like a truck.

"Yets. Much ate."

"Okay then. You're the boss. Let's go eat."

Although restaurants such as Riccardi's and Ma Raf-fa's lured in naive tourists with their fake plants and tiny white lights twinkling in their front windows, Mama took a left down a short alleyway and arrived at Rosa's, her favorite eatery in a list of winners. She turned to Brian. "This may be the only place in the world that makes better pasta than mine," she admitted.

Brian shrugged. He obviously couldn't have cared less; he was famished.

The place was dimly lit, with miniature brass lamps in the center of each white-clothed table. The pretty raven-haired host smiled at Brian, grabbed two menus and escorted them to a table in the center of the quaint dining room.

"Do you mind if we take the table in the corner?" Mama asked, pointing to the shadow under a large oil painting of the Tuscan countryside.

As the girl began to deal out the menus, she stopped and looked back.

"I can control him better if he's cornered," Mama explained with a wink, gesturing toward Brian.

The young girl laughed and led the pair to the corner of the room.

"Thank you," Mama said "And you can keep the menus. I know what we want."

They had just settled into their seats when a woman a decade older than Mama was catapulted from the kitchen's red swinging door.

"Rosa!" Mama called out as the woman approached. "Ciao, Rosa."

"Ciao, Bella," Rosa replied. She placed a basket of warm Italian flatbread and a saucer on the table—olive oil with crushed red pepper and fresh minced garlic for dipping—and then kissed Mama on each cheek. "How you, my friend?" she asked, shooting a smile toward Brian.

"Good. Good," Mama said. "Brian and I are out Christmas shopping and had to come by for a bite."

"So you bring your boyfriend today?" Rosa teased. "You on a date?"

Brian nodded. "Yets," he said, with a laugh. "Dot Mama."

"I guess that all depends on whether or not he pays," Mama joked, slapping his arm.

"You funny," Rosa said, draping a stained linen napkin over her shoulder. "Now what can I get for you?"

"Let's go with a breaded chicken cutlet for Brian, a bowl of ziti and red gravy on the side. And we'll share some stuffed cherry peppers with provolone cheese and prosciutto." She paused in thought. "How's the shrimp scampi?"

"The shrimp are as big as you head. I'll serve it on the linguine, with some romano and pecorino. *Perfecto.*" She turned and headed back toward the swinging door.

As big as my head? Mama thought. *We'll see.*

As Mama shared her favorite Christmas stories with Brian in the corner of the room, two couples sat at the bar, sharing drinks and some animated conversation. The men sipped snifters of Strega, a potent liquor that looked like lemon juice, but went down like kerosene; a witch's face smiling from the label. Their dates each enjoyed snifters of Sambuca, a licorice liquor with coffee beans floating atop. A giant copper espresso machine took up half the shelf behind the bar. Colored bottles and crystal glasses claimed the rest.

Mama was pointing out the espresso machine and trying to explain the contraption to Brian when Rosa delivered the meal. "How's you brother, Sal?" she asked. Before Mama could answer, Rosa's eyes grew distant. "Oh, I always love him." She returned to reality and looked at Mama. "Is he sick of his wife yet?"

"No, not yet," Mama said, and laughed—silently vowing to never share this conversation with her brother.

"If I only been a few years younger, we would have been family."

Mama grabbed her hand. "We are family, Rosa," she confirmed with a smile.

The woman nodded and placed the final dish on the table. "*Mangiare*...eat," she said and returned to her secret laboratory behind the red door.

Mama looked at the shrimp scampi dish and leaned into Brian's ear. "These shrimp aren't quite as big as my head," she whispered, "but they do smell delicious."

Brian nodded, but he was too busy tearing into his pasta feast to respond. His eyes told her that he knew he should answer with his words, but there was way too much chewing to be done.

Mama decided against her usual warning. *A hungry man is a hungry man*, she thought. She watched him for a moment and laughed so hard that it startled the couples at the bar. "Fine...just eat," she told him. "*Mangi.*"

When every plate on the table was clean, Rosa returned to clear the mess and deliver a steaming cappuccino for Mama and a small bowl of chocolate gelato for Brian.

"Can I get a large veal parm sandwich to go?" Mama asked. "With extra sauce."

"Sure, sure," Rosa said, pausing in thought. "Your brother always love my veal parm."

Mama nodded. "I'll let Sal know you were asking about him," she fibbed, knowing that there was no way she would ever give him the satisfaction. *I couldn't take the smirk*, she thought.

With her brother's warm sandwich in hand, Mama left a generous tip on the table and returned to their holiday adventure.

As they slowly made their way back down Hanover Street toward the Cadillac, Mama continued her tutorial on the old ways of the neighborhood. "Years ago, a lot of the things that people bought—leather jackets and new electronics—came out of the trunk of a Cadillac just like Uncle Sal's, the salesman scanning left and then right before opening his shop. Although they were the best bargains, Papa always shook his head and preferred to pay full price to an honest man. 'Only stupid people support thieves,' he'd say. 'Eventually, they'll end up buying back their own things.'

"Off this main boulevard, each side street offered a little different flavor and atmosphere—with the freshest pastas and most robust sauces in the world. The red wine and cigars were also considered the best in the city. But for a neighborhood that made much of its money from visiting diners and shoppers, outsiders were always considered suspicious and never truly welcome.

"One year, a very brave Chinese family moved in at the end of Hanover and opened a restaurant." She laughed at the memory. "No one knew how they survived because no one from the neighborhood ever ate there—or at least that's what everyone claimed. In truth, people ordered take-out and picked it up in brown paper bags from the back door, so no one could see them."

She looked around and inhaled deeply. "Yup, Little Italy has always been a unique place. While old men debated the greatness of Benito Mussolini, groups of young boys traveled like packs of wild dogs, only much better behaved. Discipline was a big deal and people took care of their own—and then some.

"There were several very well-groomed gentlemen who hung around all day dressed in suits—doing nothing. No one ever asked what they did for a living. No one needed to. A few took care of the weekly pool, while others did less. In some ways, they were like the volunteer sheriff's department. When trouble found its way into the neighborhood, before the police ever caught wind of it, these thugs would take care of it. Now that I think about it, they were more than the police. They were above the law.

"One night, after all of the children had gone to bed, a few of the well-dressed deputies dragged a young man behind the bumper of a Cadillac El Dorado. Chained by the feet, he was dragged the length of the street for trying to sell drugs in the neighborhood. Although he lived to warn others of his terrible crime, I can still hear his terrible screams..."

Mama shook off the eerie memory just as they approached Uncle Sal's car. *Maybe things aren't any worse today.* she thought. *Maybe they're just different.*

As they got in the car, Uncle Sal wiped the drool from his chin and stretched. Mama handed him his now-cold sandwich. He nodded once, and then it registered. "Did she ask about me?" he asked with a grin.

"Who?"

"You know who...Rosa!"

Mama shook her head. "Nope," she fibbed.

He studied her face and laughed. "You're full of it, Angie. She did ask about me!" he said, slapping the steering wheel in victory. "So what did you tell her?"

Mama smirked. "I told her that you always wanted her and that she should call you to set up a time to go out." She pointed out the windshield. "Now let's go home. This weather's getting bad."

He started the ignition and studied her face one last time. "You better not have told her that," he said, unwrapping his sandwich and pulling away from the curb in one fluid motion.

Mama laughed all the way to the highway.

~ ~ ~

On the ride home, more snow fell. Mama was looking toward the back seat to check on Brian when there was a loud pop. The car skidded on the slick road and veered right. Instead of slamming on the brakes, Uncle Sal pumped them lightly, while fighting the steering wheel to keep the Cadillac straight. And then there was a bang. At no more than ten miles per hour, they hit the guardrail and jolted to a stop. Mama's heart was pumping out of her chest, as she looked toward the back seat again. "You okay?" she asked, hyperventilating.

"Yets. Fun," Brian answered, his smile betraying that he'd enjoyed the experience.

She turned to Uncle Sal.

He nodded. "I'm okay. You?" he asked.

"I'm good," she lied. Somehow, she'd twisted her ankle on the floorboard and could already feel it starting to throb.

Uncle Sal jumped out of the car to survey the damage. The driver's side looked fine. He walked to the passenger side of the car. As expected, they'd had a blow out. And just as he'd dreaded, the guardrail had gouged the paint from the Cadillac's front fender right down to the back door. He shook his head and looked toward Mama.

She rolled down the window. "How bad's the damage?" she asked.

"It's nothing that can't be fixed," he yelled back, and then headed for the trunk to grab the spare. "Just a really expensive veal parm sandwich, that's all," he muttered under his breath.

~ ~ ~

Twenty miles away, Steph escorted Lauren into TA Restaurant. Though it served her favorite Portuguese food, she was more interested in ensuring that the service was impeccable. She'd called Danny Aguiar, the owner, beforehand to ensure that Lauren would be treated like royalty.

Amid the smooth and comfortable conversation, they started with giant clams—called little necks—in garlic and olive oil. Without thinking, Steph dunked her bread in the sauce and cursed herself as the treat hit her lips. *Real classy, stupid!* When Lauren quickly joined her, though, any awkwardness between them was erased. She now felt completely at ease.

As they ate, Steph tried not to gawk at Lauren, but the woman's dark, flowing hair and shining eyes didn't make it easy. She also had a rich olive complexion and a body that was well put together, making Steph fumble with some of her words.

As they both sipped red wine, Lauren explained, "I work as a behavioral therapist with troubled children," and shared many of the heart-wrenching stories that went with it. Steph hung onto every word.

For dinner, Steph had the house steak served with a fried egg and hand-cut French fries. Lauren went with the Shrimp Mozambique, a spicy dish served over white rice. Steph suggested that they wait until after the show to have dessert. Lauren agreed.

After leaving a generous tip and helping Lauren with her jacket, they headed off to the Opera House in Boston. *The Phantom of the Opera's* haunting voice was beckoning.

The beautiful theater was not how Steph remembered it. She'd been in such awe on her first visit. Tonight, she hardly noticed the majesty that surrounded them. Instead, she couldn't take her eyes off of Lauren. The show seemed to last minutes.

As they stepped onto the snow-covered sidewalk, Steph turned to her. "We could go for a drink at that jazz club that just opened, or..."

"...or we could just go for a nice walk," Lauren quickly suggested, gesturing that Steph lead the way.

Ten steps into their stroll, Steph held out her hand and felt Lauren's fingers intertwine with hers. Under a crescent moon, they walked and talked and started their beautiful descent into love. "Okay, so enough about me," Lauren said. "Tell me everything about you..."

Steph was born again.

They talked about everything and nothing at all. Steph admitted, "I've thought about finding the right person for a long time, but I think I needed to feel comfortable in my own skin before that was ever going to happen."

"Well, do you?" Lauren asked.

"Do I...what?"

"Feel comfortable in your own skin?"

Steph grinned. "I'm definitely getting there."

"Good...because you should." She smiled. "You have beautiful skin."

Steph blushed.

"So what kind of things would you do...once you found that right person?"

"Everything!"

"Tell me," she said, leaning in toward Steph, and making her swallow hard.

Steph looked into her eyes. "That's easy...fancy dinners and nights at the theater where we can sit side-by-side and hold hands. Rainy nights and old movies. Reading to each other on the beach and some skinny-dipping when the sun goes down. Getaway weekends at a bed and breakfast up north. Playing with each other's feet beneath restaurant tables."

Lauren stepped on Steph's foot and playfully raised her eyebrows.

Steph chuckled. "Hiking and camping and sleeping beneath the stars out in the middle of nowhere. Preparing dinner for two. Sharing secrets and dreams...everything. Skiing and snowmobiling in the winter. Horseback riding and vacations...away. Nostalgic afternoons of roller-skating. Sexy dresses and nights out on the town, dancing. Rock concerts in the spring. Picking apples and pumpkins in the fall. Snowball fights in December and water balloon fights in July. Laughing...lots of laughing. Getaway lunches and late night snacks and..."

Lauren stopped and turned to face Steph. "You realize that this list will take years to complete, right?"

Steph nodded and stared into her eyes. "I hope so."

"Me, too," Lauren whispered, and then closed her eyes. It was only for a moment, but she definitely closed them. When she opened them, she looked at Steph, smiled sweetly—and then winked.

Steph gasped. A chill traveled the length of her spine, while goose bumps covered her body. She pictured her tiny grandmother's smiling face. *Thank you, Mama,* she thought, while an equal amount of gratitude and excitement coursed through her veins. *You were right. Christmas wishes do come true!*

Lauren grabbed her arm, bringing her back into the present. "For now, what do you think about sharing some chocolate fondue, with those dipping strawberries and bananas?"

Steph nodded. "I think that sounds perfect."

~ ~ ~

In Mama's cottage, Brian opened his eyes to see his elderly grandmother standing there, her tiny silhouette framed in a soft light. "Did you have fun on our little adventure today?" she asked.

Brian lifted his head off the pillow and nodded.

"Use your words, Brian," she reminded him.

"Yets," he said with a smile. There was a pause. "Nigh nigh, Mama," he yawned and drifted off to sleep.

Mama tucked the covers under his chin. "Goodnight, Brian," she said, kissing his forehead and then shutting off the light.

Mama returned to the kitchen, filled the tea kettle with water and placed it on the stove. *This might be a long night,* she thought, worried about Steph being out in the bad weather.

She limped to the window and watched as the snow began falling even heavier. *Oh, Lord...please...*

The telephone rang, interrupting her silent prayer. She answered it by the second ring.

"Hi, Mama." It was Steph.

"Oh, thank God, sweetheart. I've been worried about you being out in this weather," she said, peeling herself away from the window.

"Well, you don't need to worry about me tonight, Mama," Steph said, her voice overflowing with joy.

Mama smiled. "Sounds like you took that big step of faith, huh?"

Steph giggled. "I'd say it was more like a free fall!"

Mama placed her hand over her heart. "Good for you."

There was a pause. "Thank you, Mama," Steph said, her voice choked with emotion.

"For what?" the old lady asked.

"For the best Christmas gift I've ever received."

This time, Mama had to pause. "I didn't give you anything. You gave it all to yourself."

"That's not true, Mama. You've taught me about love, without conditions or judgment. And you also taught me about faith...the kind that makes Christmas wishes come true."

Mama grabbed her crucifix and kissed it. "Love, without conditions...is there any other kind?" she asked.

"For some people," she answered.

"Then it's not real love, is it?" the old lady countered—never expecting an answer, or needing one. "So it looks like you'll be having a Merry Christmas this year..."

"I already have, Mama," Steph said, with a peaceful sigh. "I love you, you know."

"I know," Mama said. "I can feel it."

The Tin-Foil Manger

For Memere, Pepere, Mom, Aunt Jeanne and Aunt
Lorna

Chapter 1

"Mrs. Guillmette, you need to eat something to keep your strength up," Jeanne said in a gentle voice. In her twenty years as a geriatric nurse, she'd witnessed too many elderly patients simply give up, choosing death over another miserable day of life. *But not this sweet soul,* she decided, *not on my watch.*

Suffering from the onset of dementia—along with the aches and pains that were the price of a lengthy life—Nancy Guillmette was slowly wilting away in the full-care facility. "I'm dying," the frail woman whispered, as though she were sharing some unknown secret, "and that's okay. Lord knows I'm ready to go." She shook her white head. "I just never thought it would take this long."

Jeanne grinned at the old woman's beautiful spirit. "Well, while you're still here with us," she said, "why don't we make the most of each day you're given?"

Nancy stared off into space for a long moment. "What day is it, dear?"

"It's Thursday," Jeanne answered, checking her digital watch to confirm she was correct.

"Thursday…isn't that when…" She clearly lost her train of thought. Frustrated, she shook her head again.

"Your daughters are scheduled to visit today," Jeanne announced.

"My daughters?"

"Yes, Teresa and Lorna," Jeanne reminded her.

"Oh, right…. When's the last time I've seen them?"

Jeanne considered choosing kindness over truthfulness. She picked the latter. "It's been a few months, Mrs. Guillmette, but they're always sending care packages and…."

Nancy sighed heavily, cutting Jeanne off.

"Will you please eat something for me?" Jeanne asked, dangling the spoon in front of the small woman's mouth—much like Mrs. Guillmette's mother must have seventy-odd years before.

Nancy reacted like a small child, clamping her mouth shut. While her lips turned pencil-thin, she closed her eyes and shook her head from side to side.

"Oh, Mrs. Guillmette, please don't make the doctor order a feeding tube," Jeanne pled. "It would be awful for the both of us."

Nancy slowly opened her eyes, a mischievous smirk working its way into the corners of her mouth. This glimpse of consciousness, however, disappeared as quickly as it had appeared. "What day is it, dear?" she asked again.

"It's Thursday, Mrs. Guillmette, and your girls are coming to see you today."

"Girls?" she asked, her forehead creasing from confusion. "What girls?"

~ ~ ~

Teresa stepped into the dayroom with her younger sister Lorna following closely on her high heels. Amongst a sea of moaning patients, she spotted an ancient woman sitting off in a corner; the lady was slumped over, almost sulking. *There's Mom*, she realized, *staring off into nothingness.*

Slowly approaching, Teresa took a seat beside her mother's wheelchair. "Mom, it's me, she said. "And Lorna's right here with me." Her tone was louder than she'd intended.

As if awakened from a coma, her mother's head snapped up. She looked at Teresa and then over at Lorna, not a hint of recognition registering in her gray-blue eyes.

"How are you feeling, Mom?" Lorna asked, as though she also presumed the woman was deaf.

There was silence.

"We've been told you've been giving the staff a hard time, refusing to eat," Teresa said. "You need to…"

"I used to love the carnival," her mother interrupted. "Do you work in a carnival?"

Ugh, Teresa thought, realizing she was about to embark on another out-of-body experience with this skeleton who'd once been her mother.

"I like cotton candy," the old woman babbled, "and candy corn."

"You really like candy," Lorna commented. She was not teasing their mother, but attempting kindness.

For a moment, the old lady stared off into space. When she returned her attention to them, there was a sense of reality behind her ancient eyes.

There you are, Teresa thought.

Nancy's eyes started to tear up.

"What is it, Mom?" Lorna asked.

Overcome with emotion, the brittle woman fought to take in a few deep breaths—until she was able to speak. "I...I don't know," she managed, her voice now sounding like it belonged to a little girl.

"Why?" Teresa asked, preparing to stand in defense.

"I don't like... I like..." She looked back at her daughters again, her face instantly filling with terror. Her wrinkled, paper-thin hands began to tremble before her frightened eyes grew distant again.

Oh no, Teresa thought, *she's already gone.*

"Please don't..." her mother pleaded. "I'm sorry if I..." She then screamed out—as loud as her frail body would allow—sounding like a broken teakettle.

"Okay, Mom," Lorna told her over the screech. "We're going to leave now."

Two male orderlies rushed to their mother's aid, trying to help alleviate the suffering woman's child-like fears, while Teresa and Lorna melted into the shadows.

~ ~ ~

Nurse Jeanne met the middle-aged sisters in the waiting room.

"She's getting even worse," Lorna said, her voice thick with emotion.

Jeanne nodded. "It's a progressive disease and your mom's definitely taken a downward turn over these past few months."

Teresa's spine tingled, certain that the nurse was passing judgment on her and her sister's lengthy absences. She bit her tongue.

"As you know, your mother's been refusing to eat," Jeanne explained, "but in the past few days, she's also been trying to avoid taking her medications."

"Oh no," Teresa said.

Jeanne nodded. "Her dementia is creating a reality that flashes in and out…"

"…like a television with a frayed power cord," Lorna added, surprising them all.

"Exactly," Jeanne said, "but the more we're able to exercise her mind by having her recall past memories, the more effective we'll be at slowing down the process."

"We appreciate that," Teresa said, "but it's not like you can reverse this, right?"

"True," Jeanne said, "but we can slow it down. And at this point, it's not about increasing her life span; it's more about increasing her quality of life."

Lorna nodded, vigorously.

"I'm surprised she can remember anything at all," Teresa said, filled with many dark emotions.

"Listen, I was hoping you could help me," Jeanne said.

Lorna jumped in. "Of course, but how?"

"By telling me what your mom loved during her life—I mean really loved. The more insight I have, the better I can help her."

"Christmas," Teresa blurted. "She's always loved Christmas."

"That's right," Lorna agreed. "Since we were little girls, Mom loved telling us about the different holiday traditions that people celebrate all over the country."

"All over the world, really," Teresa said.

"Do you remember whether she shared these traditions with you from a book?" Jeanne asked.

Teresa shook her head. "Not at all. And that's the thing—our mother had the sharpest memory. Everything she told us—and she taught us about holiday traditions each year—she shared from memory."

"Yeah," Lorna said, "From what she told us, our grandparents filled her mind with all of it when she was young."

"And she never forgot it," Teresa added.

"That's perfect!" Jeanne said, excitedly. "This may be exactly what I need to help her slow the disease."

"Can you really do that?" Teresa asked, feeling skeptical.

"Absolutely," Jeanne confirmed, "but it takes some real time working with her."

Lorna immediately looked down, while Teresa glanced away for a moment. She felt the same tingle travel the length of her spine. But she was also confused, recognizing that this woman was genuinely concerned about her mother and equally vested toward helping her.

"It's my job," Jeanne said, wearing a disarming smile, "and I love my job."

"That's good," Lorna said.

"It sure is," Teresa agreed. "So when can we visit with her again?"

"Can you come back this afternoon? Your mom usually does better in the afternoon. I'm sure she'd love…"

"We'll be back," Teresa said, cutting her off. "We'll go grab something to eat, maybe do a little Christmas shopping, and then we'll be back." She looked at her sister.

Lorna nodded. "Lunch sounds good, though I'm not sure I feel up to doing any shopping."

Teresa half-shrugged. "Whatever," she mumbled before looking back toward the nurse. "We'll be back this afternoon," she repeated.

~ ~ ~

"Are you feeling better?" Jeanne asked a few hours later.

Nancy nodded.

"It's because you've finally taken your meds, Mrs. Guillmette."

She nodded again.

"Now, if I could only convince you to take a few bites of food. Veronica really outdid herself in the kitchen this morning. Trust me, she made a batch of split-pea soup that you don't want to miss."

Nancy placed her arthritic hand on top of Jeanne's. "I appreciate what you're doing for me, dear, I do... but aren't your efforts wasted on someone who doesn't have much time left?"

Jeanne placed her free hand on top of Nancy's. "We're all going to pass on from this world, Mrs. Guillmette," she said in a quiet voice. "But I've always believed that it's much better to be content and at peace when it's time to go." She shrugged. "I've been with many people as they've passed over. It doesn't have to be frightening or miserable, you know."

"I'm not scared," the old lady vowed.

"I know that," Jeanne whispered, "but you haven't made peace with it, either." She looked up to see Teresa and Lorna standing in the dayroom's doorway, holding wrapped presents. *Now that's odd,* she thought, *Christmas is more than a week away.*

~ ~ ~

Teresa and Lorna approached their mother, each carrying a Christmas present. *Looks like Mom's returned to the present,* Lorna thought, *enough to receive visitors, anyway.* "Hi Mom," she said, "it's your daughters, Lorna and Teresa."

The emaciated woman moaned like the ghost she was becoming.

"Do you know who we are?" Teresa asked at nearly a yell.

Nancy rocked back and forth, her eyes glaring at both of them. "Yeah, I know who you are," she hissed. "You're my long-lost daughters."

"Oh, here we go," Teresa blurted.

Lorna cringed, thinking, *At least she's cognizant.* Taking a seat beside the old woman, she said, "We brought you your Christmas presents, Mom."

"Well, isn't that nice," her mother replied sarcastically.

"We were here earlier, but you were..." Teresa stopped. "Anyway, we went out for lunch and..."

"...and we went shopping for your presents," Lorna quickly added, trying to get it in before the conversation pitched toward fantasy and reality was swallowed whole.

"Go ahead and open them," Teresa said.

Nancy never budged.

"Bob and I are taking the entire family skiing this year," Teresa reported. "We've rented a lodge in Vermont for two weeks, so I'm not sure whether I'll get a chance to see you again before the new year."

Nancy remained silent.

"And...and my kids are all coming home for the holidays," Lorna said, jumping in. "It's been years since we've all been together, so I'm really excited about having everyone under the same roof again."

"Good for you," Nancy muttered. "I can't remember all that much anymore, but I do remember when the *whole* family got together for Christmas."

"Those were the days," Lorna said, at a loss for a better reply.

"And they're long gone," Nancy added.

Teresa shook her head. "You know what, Mom," she huffed, "when we do come to see you, you're either off somewhere in your own world, or you're busting our asses and giving us a hard time. We can't win either way."

Nancy looked at Teresa, locking eyes. "That sounds like a sad story, Teresa, but you *never* come to see me. Neither of you do."

Oh Mom, Lorna thought, her heart breaking. "It's just hard, Mom," she said. "You know that. We both have families and..."

"Then you should go be with them," Nancy muttered.

Teresa stood to leave. "You don't have to tell me twice," she snapped, starting for the door.

Her eyes filling, Lorna leaned in to kiss her mother's wrinkled cheek. "I'll come by to see you around Christmas," she whispered.

"No, you won't," Nancy said. "Don't tell me that, Lorna, because we both know you won't."

Although her mother was right, Lorna had spent a decade justifying her absence from the woman's life. *My family needs me more*, Lorna told herself, standing to leave. "Merry Christmas, Mom," she said.

"No, Lorna," Nancy said, "it hasn't been a Merry Christmas for a very long time."

~ ~ ~

Jeanne waited for Mrs. Guillmette's daughters to leave before she pulled a chair in front of the woman.

"They couldn't stay long," Nancy said.

"Well, it's a busy time with everyone getting ready for the holidays," Jeanne said. "It's nice that they came to visit you."

Nancy pointed to the two wrapped presents stacked on the table beside her. "They only came here to clear the consciences," she said matter-of-factly. "They got me out of the way early; that's exactly what they did."

"Oh, Mrs. Guillmette, that can't be true," Jeanne fibbed.

"But it is," Nancy said. "You know, I spent most of my life raising those selfish girls all by myself. And as far as they're concerned, I'm already lying six feet under."

"Mrs. Guillmette," Nancy repeated, both words dripping with empathy. "But you're not dead, are you? You're still here. And so am I, sitting right here with you."

Nancy peered into Jeanne's eyes before squeezing her hand. "You're a good soul, Jeanne, do you know that?"

"And so are you, which is why I want you to remember all the joys you've experienced in your life."

Nancy chuckled, which immediately turned into a cough. "My goodness, I can't even recall the last conversation that you and I shared."

"I realize that. But long-term memory works differently than short-term memory," the nurse explained, "and that's what I'd like to start working on with you."

"How?" Nancy asked, revealing her first glimmer of interest.

"By just talking," Jeanne answered, smiling wide. "That's all."

"Talking? About what?"

"I was thinking we could start by remembering some Christmases that have passed."

Nancy's face lit up. "Oh, I used to love Christmas."

"That's what I've heard," Jeanne said, still beaming. "So let's see if we can't get some of those same feelings back for you." She raised an eyebrow. "What do you say?"

Nancy half-shrugged. "I guess we can try," she muttered. "It's not like I have anything better to do."

Jeanne laughed. "Okay then, we'll start tomorrow... just as soon as you eat some breakfast."

"I have to warn you, though," Nancy said, "you're not going to hear any stories about silver spoons or golden slippers." Wearing the first genuine smile Jeanne had witnessed on the affable woman, Nancy nodded. "We were so poor that my family actually ate the fruitcake when we received one."

Jeanne laughed. "I'm going to enjoy our story time together, aren't I?"

"I hope so," Nancy said, "as long as I can remember any..."

"You will," Jeanne said, confidently. "And please don't worry about being judged. Whatever you tell me..."

"Oh, no worries there, sweetheart," Nancy said, "If I cared at all about what other people thought, I could've never been me."

"Perfect," Jeanne said, nodding, "then we're starting at the right place."

Chapter 2

Although they were only days away from Christmas, Nancy Guillmette was miserable, lacking any spirit whatsoever for the holiday. For her, the season had long lost its magic.

"So you used to really love Christmas, huh?" Jeanne said. "What do you think changed that?"

"It's too commercial now," Nancy complained, "with toy advertisements running in November." She shook her head, sadly. "Most of my family and friends, the folks I really loved, have passed away," She half-shrugged. "I suppose it's the price owed for living a long life." She shook her white crop of hair again. "And you've met my daughters. No need to say any more there."

"But Mrs. Guillmette, some people..."

"It's my own doing," the old lady interrupted. "I take full responsibility. When you spoil children rotten, you end up with rotten adults. There's no great mystery there."

"Okay," Jeanne said.

"In my opinion," Nancy said, moving beyond the awkward moment, "people who don't celebrate Christmas are trying to ruin it for the rest of us who do. No matter what you celebrate, it shouldn't be about exclusion; it should be about inclusion—embracing all holiday traditions from every religion." She shrugged. "When you get right down to it, none of us is really that different at all. We all need to be loved and treated with kindness, right?"

"Absolutely," Jeanne said. "Why don't we talk about what Christmas was like when you were a kid?"

"That was a different lifetime ago," Nancy muttered, sadly.

"I'd love to hear about it," Jeanne prodded.

"You would, huh?" The old woman grinned.

Jeanne matched her smile. "I would."

"So where do I begin?" Nancy asked, clearly unsure about this request.

"As far back as you can remember," Jeanne said, "and don't leave anything out. I want to know every detail."

"And...and what if I can't...you know...remember?" Nancy asked in the voice of a frightened child.

"You will, Mrs. Guillmette," Jeanne promised. "Just don't force it." She grabbed Nancy's hand. "Just let it come to you, okay?"

Nancy took a deep breath and then another before she closed her eyes. She stayed there for a long while, never moving an inch. Suddenly, she grinned. A moment later, the grin transformed into a full-blown smile. "I was young, really young," she said, excitedly, "I remember trudging down Eastern Avenue in a snowstorm holding my papa's hand. Garland was strung from one lamppost to the next in a zigzag pattern, with giant wreaths hanging right above the street."

With a heavy sigh of relief, she sprinted back to her joyful childhood.

~ ~ ~

Small white lights illuminated the trees that retained a hint of green. Cars—with pine trees secured to their roofs with rope—slipped down the slushy street. Children were bundled against the bitter cold, scarves concealing everything but wide eyes peering out. Without fail, one of the kids would always hit Papa's car with a snowball. And he'd always stop and pretend to give chase, balling up snow and throwing it back at the kids. *He laughed so hard doing that,* Nancy recalled. They'd stop for cups of hot chocolate, while the festive music of Nat King Cole swooned in the background. *If Papa had his way, though, we'd be listening to Elvis Presley's* Blue Christmas *album.*

The air was cold, and little Nancy got a kick out of the steam that escaped her mouth when she talked. *It looks like I'm smoking just like Papa.* The sky was dark, but a pretty dark—gray mixed with splashes of pink and purple. "Feels like more snow's coming," Papa would say before turning up the collar on his woolen coat. He was like a fortuneteller because, not two minutes later, Nancy watched as the first snowflake fluttered to the ground—and then another. A minute later, there were thousands dancing around in the air, tickling her red button nose and blanketing the filthy ground.

After stopping at Jack and Harry's—an old five-and-dime department store—to buy Mama's Christmas gift, they returned home to the distinct smell of cinnamon filling the house. "Mama's making her magic in the kitchen," Papa said before taking a knee in front of the fireplace. Within minutes, small orange flames began licking the cold out of the living room.

Mama came out of the kitchen, wiping her hands on her faded red-and-green-striped apron, leaving behind two white-flour handprints. "So where did you two go?" she asked, looking directly at Nancy.

Nancy half-opened her mouth before looking toward her father for help.

"It's our secret, Louise," Papa said, "and you'll have to wait until Christmas to find out." He added a few more sticks of wood onto the growing flames before taking a seat in his worn armchair. He looked at Nancy. "What time is it?" he asked, grinning.

"Story time, right, Papa?" she answered, hopefully.

After a firm nod, he grabbed his thick Christmas book from the end table on his left. "That's right," he said, flipping open the front cover. "Now where did we leave off last?"

"You started telling us about Christmas holly, but you never finished," Nancy reminded him.

"Ah, that's right, baby girl," Papa said, skimming through the book until he found his place. "'Many years ago,'" he read, "'in northern Europe, people believed that ghosts and demons could be heard howling on the winter winds. They also believed that boughs of holly had magical powers because they were one of the few things that remained green throughout the harsh winters.'"

"I have a friend named, Holly," Nancy said. "She wants to be a hairdresser when she grows up."

"She must be lucky, right?" her mother commented, sitting in her chair, mending clothes.

"I don't think so," Nancy said. After giving it some thought, she shook her head. "Holly gets picked last when we play games at school and she always has some sort of rash on her neck."

"Sorry to hear all of that," her papa said, while Mama laughed.

"Anyway," Papa continued, "boughs of holly were often placed over the doors of homes, in the hopes of driving away evil spirits."

"That's not good," Nancy said, nervously.

"Greenery was also brought indoors to freshen the air and brighten the mood during the long, dreary winters," Papa added, hurrying to get past the scary part. He looked up from his book. "And that's the real reason that we still decorate with it today."

Nancy nodded, relieved. "Well, holly looks nice enough, but I cut myself on one of the leaves last year when we were making wreaths in class."

"Then maybe you're right," her papa teased. "Maybe holly's not so lucky, after all."

Mama laughed again.

"Tell me another story, Papa," Nancy begged. "Please tell me another one."

As Papa stood, he moaned once before grabbing for the small of his back. Slowly approaching the fireplace, he used the black steel poker to push around the glowing embers. When he was finished, he grabbed for one of the red stockings that hung from the mantle. "What are these stinky socks doing here?" he asked.

Nancy laughed excitedly. "Those aren't stinky, Papa. We leave them for Santa every year!"

"Why, he doesn't have his own socks?" the grinning man asked.

"We put them there so he'll put presents and candy in them."

Papa eased back into his chair. "Oh, that's right," he said, opening his Christmas book again. "'According to the legend, the tradition of the Christmas stockings began with a kind English nobleman who had three daughters. The nobleman's wife passed on, leaving her husband and their daughters very sad—not to mention having to do all the work in the house. When the daughters became eligible for marriage, the poor father could not afford to give huge dowries that any future husband might expect at the time.'" He shook his head for drama's sake. "'One evening, after washing their stockings, the daughters hung them near the fireplace to be dried. Santa Claus—being moved by their loss—put a bag of gold into each one of the stockings hanging by the chimney. The next morning, the family noticed the gold bags and the nobleman had enough for his daughter's marriage. The daughters got married and they lived happily ever after.'"

"And children have been hanging Christmas stockings ever since," her mama added, looking up from her sewing.

"So you guys always hung stockings for Santa, too?" Nancy asked.

"Well, not exactly," Papa said. "We used our shoes and placed them by the fireplace on Christmas Eve."

"Shoes?" Nancy repeated.

"In France, children place their shoes by the fireplace in hopes that Père Noël will leave gifts for them," Mama explained. "Nearly every French home at Christmastime displays a Nativity scene, and the French make a traditional Yule cake called the Christmas Log."

"Candy in shoes?" Nancy repeated. "Yuck!"

Her papa chuckled. "Actually, not for candy. The best we could ever hope for was a few figs and an orange."

"Man, am I glad I was born here," Nancy said.

Her mama laughed. "Not me," she said. "I wouldn't have traded those figs for all the stocking stuffers in the world."

"You know, I really am happy that we celebrate Christmas in America," Nancy said after giving it some more thought.

"Still stuck on the figs in the shoes, huh?" Papa said.

Nancy shrugged.

~ ~ ~

As though she were emerging from a dream; a dream that had once been her life, Nancy opened her swollen eyes. "Christmas was always such a special time. Papa was home and not at work, where he usually spent most of his time." She nodded. "The family was home—together—you know?"

"I do," Jeanne whispered.

"Papa had an account at a small department store on Eastern Avenue. The place carried everything from sweaters to sleds. Papa would take me there to buy Mama's Christmas present. It was never anything big, but obviously more than we could afford because he visited the place every Friday to make his weekly payment until the gift was paid off months later."

Jeanne smiled at the warm memory.

"And I made a snowman every year," Nancy said, excited to share her long-lost memories, "which usually lacked the outerwear that other families dressed theirs in. Of course, I'd give them rocks for eyes and a mouth, and a carrot nose...until some wild animal chewed it off him."

Jeanne laughed.

"Papa also made a fire in the fireplace each night," Nancy rambled on, taking a deep breath. "I loved the smells of burnt wood and was hypnotized by the dancing red and orange flames. I could watch them for hours, and sometimes did—until Mama called me away, having me join her in the kitchen to do some cooking and baking." She looked at Jeanne. "There were never many sweets around the house during the year, so I loved it when we baked."

"I can understand that," Jeanne said.

"I remember my mama's homemade bread...eating it warm, with globs of butter melting right down to the crust."

"Mrs. Guillmette, you're making my mouth water," Jeanne said.

Nancy licked her thin lips.

"What do you say we each grab a bite to eat for lunch?" Jeanne asked.

Nancy shook her head. "I think I'll pass...unless you can get your hands on my mama's homemade bread."

"Oh, Mrs. Guillmette," Jeanne sighed. "You really do need to eat."

Nancy closed her eyes again. "There are different ways we can nourish ourselves, dear," she whispered.

"I agree," Jeanne said, "but without proper sustenance, those other ways mean very little."

Chapter 3

Jeanne brought in a loaf of warm bread, lathered in butter. She approached Nancy to hand her a piece when she realized something was amiss.

"When is my mom coming to pick me up?" Nancy asked.

"What's that, Mrs. Guillmette?" Jeanne questioned, realizing, *She's missed her meds again.*

"My mama...she's supposed to come and pick me up after school." Nancy started to fidget, her nervousness quickly changing to panic, widening her eyes.

"You're fine, Mrs. Guillmette," Jeanne promised. "We just need to take your medication."

"I don't want any pills," Nancy said, putting her hand over her mouth.

"It's time for your pills. In fact, you're past due. Trust me, you'll feel much better once you take them."

Nancy lifted her hand an inch from her mouth, leaving it there in defense. "My papa doesn't like me accepting anything from strangers." She began to cry, mournfully. "Please, lady," she pleaded, "please don't make me." The sorrowful crying continued.

~ ~ ~

Several hours had passed when Jeanne spotted Nancy's wheelchair parked near the window, facing the gray sky outside. "Are you feeling any better, Mrs. Guillmette?" she asked in a soft voice intended not to startle.

The old woman looked at her with bright eyes, fully in the present. "Of course," she said, oblivious to the difficult morning she'd experienced. "As good as can be expected, I suppose."

With a compassionate nod, Jeanne said, "Looks like a dark day out there."

"Looks like snow," Nancy quickly countered, her eyes back on the window. "There's nothing more magical than the calm before it starts. It's like the world stops spinning for a brief moment."

After agreeing with her patient, Jeanne cleared her throat. "I wanted to tell you that you've inspired me to research even more holiday traditions," she said.

"How wonderful," the elder said.

"Do you want to hear them?"

"Of course."

Nodding, Jeanne began to ramble off the new information, hoping that Nancy would be able to retain just a fraction of it. "In Washington D.C., a huge tree is lit by the president, and New York City lights up one that's even bigger at Rockefeller Center. In Boston, right up the road from us, carolers sing on street corners, many playing hand bells. And in New Orleans, a huge ox is paraded around the streets decorated with holly and with ribbons tied to its horns."

"That's great," Nancy said, "I visited New Orleans once. But it was in the summer." She shook her head. "It's so humid down there."

Jeanne nodded before going on. "In parts of New Mexico, at Christmastime, people place lighted candles in paper bags filled with sand on streets and rooftops to light the way for the Christ Child. In Arizona, the

Mexican ritual called *Las Posadas* is a procession and play representing the search of Mary and Joseph for a room at the inn. Families play the parts and visit each other's houses, enacting and re-enacting the drama, while admiring each other's' nativity scenes."

"Ahhh, the nativity," Nancy cooed.

"In Colorado," Jeanne said, "an enormous star is placed on the mountain, where it can be seen for many miles around. And in Philadelphia, a procession called the Mummers Parade runs for a whole day with bands, dancers and people in fancy costumes."

"That's fantastic," Nancy said, genuinely impressed.

Jeanne waited a few moments. "Mrs. Guillmette, do you remember what animal they parade around the streets in New Orleans during Christmas?"

Nancy's brow furrowed as she searched her mind for the correct answer.

"They decorate the animal in holly and ribbons," Jeanne added, offering a clue.

Nancy shook her head. "I don't know, sweetheart. I'm sorry," she said. "But did you know that in Northern Europe, boughs of holly were once placed over the doors of homes in the hopes of driving away evil spirits?"

Wearing a kind smile, Jeanne nodded. "I recently heard that," she said, leaving it there.

Suddenly, the first few snowflakes floated down in front of the window.

Nancy smiled. "I used to love when it snowed around Christmastime…"

Without further prodding, she went back in time.

~ ~ ~

Leafless trees stood stark against the charcoal night, their bare branches encased in Mother Nature's transparent lacquer. The world was covered in white, the occasional human leaving tire tracks or footprints in their wake. Both were covered within minutes, as though no one had ever disturbed the scene. The street lamps' soft light illuminated the crystallized scene, shimmering and sparkling. Shop windows, partially obstructed by the frost creeping out from their corners, faced the mounds of dirty snow piled up in the gutters that abutted the disappearing curbs. Everything was barren and frozen outside; everything warm and inviting inside those shop windows. Beneath the telephone lines, sagging low from the weight of the heavy ice, the Guillmette family headed home with their pathetic-looking Christmas tree.

"I really love hearing about all the different holiday traditions, Papa," Nancy said, kicking off her boots in the mudroom.

"Me, too," her mama agreed, watching as her grunting husband wrestled the frozen tree into the warm house.

"Me, three," Papa said, "and no matter where you're from, storytelling has been one of those holiday traditions for centuries." He spent the next ten minutes trying to straighten the tree in the rickety old tree stand.

"Can we decorate it tonight?" Nancy asked.

"Not until Christmas eve, baby girl," Papa said, trying to catch his breath, "you know that."

"Besides, the tree needs to settle and open up a little before we can dress it," Mama added.

"Why don't we learn about more holiday traditions instead?" Papa asked, brushing pine needles off his shirt and pants and taking a seat in his armchair by the dancing fire.

"Yes!" Nancy said, joyfully. "I love how people celebrate the holiday season so differently," Nancy said.

"I do, too," Papa agreed, grabbing for his thick book. "And as you travel around the globe, it gets even more amazing." He took a few breaths before he began to read. "In China, some people light their houses with beautiful paper lanterns and decorate their Christmas trees— which they call Trees of Light—with paper chains and paper flowers. Chinese children hang stockings in hopes that Santa Claus will fill them with treats."

"See," Nancy said, "they hang stockings, too."

Papa nodded. "In England, Boxing Day is celebrated the first weekday after Christmas, when small gifts or coins are given to anyone who comes calling. And Christmas in Australia is usually very hot. While we're in the middle of winter, Australians are baking in the summer heat on the other side of the world."

"A flaming Christmas plum pudding is their tradition," Mama added from memory, "and small presents are baked inside some of them. They believe that whoever finds the presents will enjoy good luck that year."

"I doubt my friend Holly would find any of those presents," Nancy said.

Mama and Papa both laughed.

"In India, houses are decorated with strings of mango leaves," Papa continued. "Lights are placed on the window sills and walls and a star is hung outside. A sweet holiday treat called *thali* is made and brought to neighbors and friends."

"Sharing with neighbors," her mama muttered. "Good for them."

"In some parts of India," Papa added, "small clay oil-burning lamps are used as Christmas decorations, and are placed on the edges of flat roofs and on the tops of walls."

"Now that's different," Nancy commented.

"In Sweden," Papa said, "on Santa Lucia Day, at first light, the oldest daughter of the family dresses in white and wears a wreath of seven candles on her head. It is her job to wake the rest of the family and serve them coffee, buns, and cookies. The Swedish have another custom where a gift is wrapped in many layers of paper. They then knock on someone's door and leave the present there. The longer it takes someone to open the gift, the better."

"I like that one," Nancy said.

"And when I was your age," Louise told Nancy, "I learned from my Portuguese friend that her family enjoyed a feast called *consoada*, where they set extra places at the table for the souls of the dead. They eat codfish and sweet rice, and they set up a Nativity scene," she added, her voice betraying jealousy, "with Mary, Joseph, the three wise man, and all the barn animals."

"Codfish and sweet rice," Nancy repeated, unsure about the strange combination.

Mama stood. "And many of these foreign traditions are carried over when families move to America," she added before heading out of the room to make hot cocoa.

Papa nodded. "That's right. On Christmas Eve, Polish Americans spread hay on their kitchen floor and under the tablecloth to remind them of a stable and a manger. When they make up the table for dinner, two extra places are set for Mary and the Christ Child—in case they should knock at the door to ask for shelter."

"I love that," Nancy said, giving it some thought.

"No matter where we come from, most people believe that this is the season for giving," Papa said.

Just then, Mama returned with three steaming mugs of hot cocoa. "And for thinking about people other than ourselves," she added.

"And you don't need to have money to give—right, Mama?" Nancy said.

Mama smiled. "That's right, sweetheart. The most precious gifts don't cost anything... except maybe your time and a willingness to help others." She nodded. "Believe it or not, your papa and I used to get a big group together and sing off-tune at an old folks home every year."

"And you don't anymore?" Nancy said.

Papa shook his head. "We're the old folks now," he teased. "But Mama's right, giving's not about the money at all." He skimmed through the pages of his Christmas book until he found the story he was looking for. "'There's an old Mexican legend that a young boy named Pablo was on his way to visit the village Nativity scene when he realized that he had no gift for the Christ Child. Thinking about it, he gathered some green branches along the side of the road and brought them to the church. Though the other children made fun of him, when the leaves were laid at the manger, a beautiful star-shaped flower appeared on each branch—with bright red petals." He looked up at his daughter. "Can you tell me what that holiday plant is called today, Nancy?"

"A rose?"

"Good guess, but no—it's called a poinsettia."

"But the plant's name doesn't matter," Mama interjected. "It's the message that counts."

Nodding, Nancy internalized the important lesson. "Whether you're rich or poor, the best gifts in this world come straight from the heart," Mama concluded.

Nancy continued to nod, giving this concept much more thought.

~ ~ ~

The smells of cinnamon filled the nursing home, yanking Nancy back into the present. She tilted her head skyward to take in the wonderful aroma.

"Veronica's making her famous cinnamon rolls for Christmas morning," Jeanne explained.

"I've always loved the smell of cinnamon," Nancy said. "My mama used it in her gorton."

"Gah-taw?"

"It's spelled 'g-o-r-t-o-n.' It's a French pork spread. Every Christmas, my mom made it for our family and for the poor families that needed extra help around the holidays. She even delivered the meals to the church, guaranteeing her anonymity. 'It's for God to know,' she'd always tell me, 'and no one else.' This was tough to understand, though, because it wasn't that hard for me to picture our priest eating my mother's famous gorton." She grinned. "Making gorton at Christmas was an annual tradition for our family."

"I'm starting to sense that you really love holiday traditions," Jeanne teased.

Nancy's smile grew. "I can't remember what I ate for my last breakfast, but I still know how to make my mother's gorton. Isn't that something?"

"It's normal, Mrs. Guillmette." She leaned in close. "So you still remember how to make gorton, huh?"

"I do," Nancy said, proudly.

"Then let's hear it?"

"Sorry, sweetheart, it's a secret family recipe," Nancy said, her mischievous eyes shining as if they belonged to a young woman again.

"My lips are sealed," Nancy promised.

Nancy closed her eyes and began counting on her crooked fingers. "Place the pork, onion, cinnamon, and clove into a saucepan. Season to taste with salt and pepper. Pour in water...just enough to cover the meat. Bring to a boil over high heat, then reduce the heat to medium-low, cover, and cook until the water has nearly evaporated." She thought for a moment. "It should take about an hour. Stir occasionally, making sure the pork cooks evenly. Use a potato masher or wire whisk to break the pork into thin strands. Pour off any remaining liquid, then spoon the gorton into a serving bowl." She stopped.

"Mrs. Guillmette, that's so..." Jeanne began to say.

"Refrigerate before serving," Nancy interrupted with a smile.

"Wow," Jeanne said, truly impressed. "That's fantastic!" She leaned in even closer, whispering, "I'll never tell a soul."

Nancy laughed. "I'd prefer that you made a batch and brought some in."

Jeanne was taken aback. "I will...but only if you promise to eat it with me?"

Nancy nodded slightly. "Just go easy on the cinnamon. You can ruin it with too much."

"Good to know," Jeanne said, "I'll keep it in mind." She paused. "Is that true," Jeanne asked, "that Polish Americans spread hay on their kitchen floor and under the tablecloth on Christmas Eve to remind them of a stable and a manger?"

"According to my papa, it's true," Nancy said, her eyes misting over, "and he never once lied to me."

"Then I believe it," Jeanne said.

Chapter 4

Music filled the dayroom—Bing Crosby's "White Christmas."

"I love that song," Jeanne said. "My mom used to play her Bing Crosby album every Christmas."

"Mine, too," Nancy admitted.

"You never had any siblings, Mrs. Guillmette?" Jeanne asked, studying the woman's face.

"I had an older brother, Al, who we called Junior. However, I could say I was an only child and not be lying to you. Junior was eleven years older than me, and was already out of the house before I noticed he was gone." She grinned. "My parents said I was their blessed surprise."

"I can see that."

"I don't think Junior and I would have gotten along well, anyway. He had the social skills of an eight-year-old, which may actually be insulting to eight-year-olds everywhere."

Jeanne laughed at the woman's razor-sharp wit.

"I think my brother finished raising himself because he was emotionally immature," Nancy added, "almost like my parents hadn't finished the baking and he came out a little too doughy."

Jeanne laughed harder. "What happened to your brother?"

"He drowned doing one too many laps in the bottom of a whiskey bottle."

"I'm sorry to hear that," Jeanne said.

"Thank you, but his was not the death that destroyed my family..." She stopped.

"You can tell me," Jeanne quietly offered.

Nancy took some deep breaths to steady herself. "As a young woman, I lived a wonderful life—almost perfect—with my husband and our two little girls... that is, until we suffered a tragedy that we never got past, leaving me to raise our two girls alone."

"Oh no..." Jeanne blurted.

Whether she wanted to make the trip or not, Nancy's mind warped back to that awful day.

~ ~ ~

Excited about the upcoming weekend, twenty-five-year-old Nancy had just returned home from the market. They'd planned to take the girls to the city for their first visit to the aquarium. Curiously, Roy's faded black Buick wasn't sitting in the driveway. *That's odd,* she'd thought, *he usually beats me home on Fridays after another tough day at the construction site.* Stepping into the house, she checked the kitchen table for a note. *Nothing.* She was just picking up the telephone to call his mother's house when she spotted the black-and-white police cruiser pull into Roy's normal spot in the driveway. Her stomach sank. *Something's wrong,* she thought and hurried to the door. Randy Philips, a veteran officer and long-time friend, looked ready for tears. He approached the porch, shaking his head. Nancy felt her knees start to give. As she steadied herself, Randy cleared his throat. "Roy's been rushed to the hospital,

Nancy. He was struck by a steel girder at work and..."
Nancy rushed past the man and didn't take a full breath
until she and the girls were at the hospital.

But they were too late. Roy's body had been broken
beyond repair, his mind already beginning a sequence
of shutting down one circuit after the next. Although
his heart beat for three more days, Nancy's beloved
passed away—dying to the rhythm of his wife's broken
heart.

~ ~ ~

Nancy opened her eyes and accepted the tissue that
Jeanne handed her. "That year, along with many other
things, our Christmas traditions died with my husband." She shook her sorrowful head. "Much of the
goodness I'd known my entire life was suddenly forgotten...to include my faith."

"Oh, Mrs. Guillmette," Jeanne said. "I didn't realize..."

Nancy raised her hand, halting the kind nurse.
"How did you get into this type of work... spending
your days with old farts?" she asked, obviously needing to change the subject.

"When I was young," Jeanne explained, happy to
comply and switch directions, "my dad would take me
to the Golden Pines nursing home on Christmas Eve
to visit with the patients. We'd eat the cookies I baked
and then sing Christmas carols." Her eyes misted
over. "Those are still my favorite holiday memories."
She shrugged. "In fact, I loved them so much that it
inspired me to pursue a nursing career, working with
the elderly."

"Christmas really is a magical time, isn't it?" Nancy
commented.

"It sure is. I remember that my dad and I would go home and watch It's a Wonderful Life with…"

"With Jimmy Stewart," Nancy finished. "It's my favorite movie of all time."

"Really?" Jeanne said. "Mine, too. I love that movie's message."

"It's the best," Nancy agreed.

"You know, the more I get to know you, Mrs. Guillmette," Jeanne said, "the more I'm sure that there are many lives that wouldn't have been the same without you."

"Well, I'm not sure about that," Nancy said, humbly.

"I am. I know my life wouldn't be the same without you."

"That's sweet of you to say," Nancy said, her grayish eyes filling. "What's funny is that my papa used to say the same thing."

"I bet he did," Jeanne said, pausing for a moment. "You know; your dad sounds like he was an angel."

Nancy nodded. "He's always been my angel, that's for sure," she whispered, swallowing hard. "I remember the year he told me to write a letter to Santa Claus." The subtlest smile grew until it took up her entire face. As her eyes glassed over, she went back in time once again.

~ ~ ~

Little Nancy placed the stubby pencil onto her small, wooden desk, picked up the sheet of paper and read it slowly.

Dear Santa, I've been a good girl this year. Not perfect, but not bad. I know that mamas and papas help you sometimes to put presents under the Christmas tree. And my mama and papa don't have a lot of money, so I was hoping you could bring me my gift. Nothing big, just a dolly that I can name Susan. I've always wanted a dolly named Susan. Thank you, Mr. Claus, and Merry Christmas to you.

~ ~ ~

"Did you write a letter to Santa this year?" Mama asked a few days later.

Nancy nodded. "Papa reminded me, so I wrote it and he's already mailed it for me," she said.

"Very good because it's important that we help Santa out and let him know what we want for Christmas, right?"

Nancy nodded. "Did you and Papa write your letters to Santa this year?"

"Well, sweetheart, Santa's in the kid business," her mama cautiously answered. "He's not so much in the grown-up business."

"So you don't write letters anymore?" Nancy asked.

"Well, we do," her papa jumped in, teasing, "but they're more like love letters that we give to each other."

Her mama smiled, giving her papa the eye.

"But if you did write to Santa," Nancy said, "what would you ask him for?"

"That you get every single thing that you deserve," Mama said, nodding, "because Papa and I both know that you've been on your best behavior all year."

"Did you remember to mail my letter, Papa?" Nancy asked.

"Of course," he said, "how else would Santa Claus get it?"

Nancy giggled with glee.

"Well, in England, instead of mailing out their Christmas lists," Mama said, "children throw them into their fireplaces so that Santa can read the smoke."

"That's strange," Nancy said.

"Not strange," Mama corrected her, "just different. Right, sweetheart?"

"Right."

"So where was Santa Claus when Jesus was born?" the young girl asked. "Was he one of the wise men?"

Her mama chuckled. "No, honey; my guess is that Santa Claus was in the North Pole when Baby Jesus spent his first night on this earth."

"Santa Claus is actually Saint Nicholas from Turkey," Papa explained, "a man whose kindness, generosity and devotion to children has been celebrated by people for generations throughout the world."

"And for us in America," Mama added, "it all started with Dutch children leaving their wooden shoes by the fireplace, where Santa Claus would reward the good children by placing treats in their shoes."

"Just like our French family, right?" Nancy said, proudly.

Mama nodded. "That's right. When the Dutch came to America, they brought this tradition with them and we've been looking forward to Santa's visit every year since then."

"Wooden shoes?" Nancy said. "That's so weird."

"No, not weird, sweetheart," Mama said, "just different, remember?"

"People believe a lot of different things," Papa said. "Children in Belgium believe that Santa Claus visits them twice."

"Twice?" Nancy repeated. "That's great!"

"Yup, the first time, so that he can find out which children have been good and which ones have been bad," Papa said. "If a child is good, he returns with the presents that the good children deserve. If they were bad, he leaves them twigs inside their shoes or within the baskets that they leave just inside their doorways."

"Twigs?" Nancy said, "that's awful."

"And in Czechoslovakia, they believe that Santa Claus climbs down from heaven on a golden rope," Papa said.

"Wow, a golden rope," Nancy repeated, "that's so neat." She thought for a moment. "But it doesn't matter as long as he visits children all over the world, right?"

"That's right," Papa said, adding a wink, "or at least the good ones."

Mama nodded. "Although he's known as Father Christmas in England, *Père Noël* in France, and a hundred other names across the globe, we're all waiting on the same jolly, plump man with a white beard, hearty laugh and a thick red suit."

"Should we stop here?" Papa asked, referring to the Christmas tales.

"No, no," Nancy answered. "Keep going...please!"

Smiling, he dove back into his book. "'Children who live in Denmark believe that Santa's elves live in the attics of their homes, so they leave rice pudding and saucers of milk out for them.'"

"I love rice pudding," Mama commented.

"As long as it's not served with codfish," Nancy said. Everyone laughed.

"Russia has *Babouschka*," Papa continued, "who brings gifts for the children. The tradition says that she failed to give food and shelter to the three wise men and so she now searches the countryside, visiting children and giving gifts as she goes. And the Swedish people call Santa *Tomte* and see him as a gnome who comes out from under the floor of the house or barn, carrying his sack of gifts for them. He rides in a goat-drawn sleigh."

Nancy and Mama laughed.

"In Switzerland, Santa Claus is called *Christkind*, who—dressed in all white and a golden crown—brings gifts to the children," Papa said. "And the children of Spain leave their shoes on the windowsills filled with straw, carrots, and barley for the horses of the wise men—who, they believe, reenact their journey to Bethlehem every year. One of the wise men is called *Balthazar*, and he leaves the children gifts."

"What about in Japan?" Nancy asked.

Papa searched his book. "Ahhh," he said, "in Japan, there is a priest known as *Hoteiosho*, who looks just like our Santa Claus—a kind, old man carrying a huge pack. The children believe that he has eyes in the back of his head, so they stay on their best behavior—because he can see everything."

"Well, whoever it is that brings us presents," Nancy said, "I hope he hurries up."

Mama and Papa both laughed.

"No matter what we call him, I just wish we didn't have to wait so long," Nancy moaned.

~ ~ ~

Nancy returned to the present to see Jeanne smiling at her.

"Those really were some great stories," Jeanne said, genuinely excited.

"I agree," Nancy said, "and I remember them like they happened yesterday."

"That's fantastic, Mrs. Guillmette. I love hearing them, and I can't thank you enough for sharing them with me."

"It's my pleasure, dear, but I'm the one who should be thanking you. I feel like I'm getting to live them all over again." She clasped her wrinkled hands together. "What a gift!"

Jeanne cleared her throat. "From what I understand," she said, "holiday traditions vary from one state to the next in America. And just because we live in the same country, that doesn't mean that we all celebrate in the same ways."

"That's right, dear," Nancy agreed.

"Did you know that in Hawaii, Christmas starts with the arrival of the Christmas Tree Ship? Santa Claus also arrives by boat, and Christmas dinner is eaten outdoors."

"Really? That's wonderful."

"Yup. In California, Santa Claus sweeps in on a surfboard, and in Alaska boys and girls with lanterns on poles carry a large figure of a star from door to door. They sing carols and are usually invited in for supper."

"If they sing good enough, I'm guessing."

Jeanne laughed before searching the old woman's face. "Can you tell me how Santa Claus arrives in Hawaii to bring toys to the children there, Mrs. Guillmette?"

Nancy's smile slowly disappeared. "I don't remember Papa telling me about that one," she said, "I'm sorry."

"That's okay, Mrs. Guillmette," Jean said, kindly, "I can look it up later."

Chapter 5

It was two days before Christmas. Although Jeanne's efforts toward improving Mrs. Guillmette's short-term memory was proving futile, the joy the woman was experiencing by accessing her long-term memories was priceless.

"Mrs. Guillmette's so funny," Jeanne told one of her colleagues. "What a spirit that woman has. I can't imagine not spending every day with her if she were my mom."

"She may not be your mom, but you do spend every day with her," her fellow nurse reminded her.

"That's true." Jeanne smiled. "I'm so lucky."

"And so is she."

"Thanks."

~ ~ ~

Jeanne marveled at the magical transformation: Mrs. Guillmette's hair was now brushed, she was sporting a colorful Christmas sweater and, best of all, she now wore a smile that threatened to become permanent.

Without being asked, the elderly matron now reveled in her age-old memories. "Every Christmas Eve, my family would trim the Christmas tree by stringing popcorn and cranberries, as well as gingerbread cookies," Nancy said. "It really was an edible giving tree."

"That's nice," Jeanne said.

"We always adopted the scrawniest, most pathetic Christmas trees you ever saw. We used tinsel, lots of tinsel, and also angel's hair, which I believe was fiberglass, to fill any of the big holes in the tree."

"I've never heard of angel's hair."

"That's a good thing. Then you're probably not at risk for emphysema."

Jeanne laughed.

"They used to let me put the star on top of the tree," Nancy said.

"A star, huh?"

"Never anything but." Nancy shook her head, sadly. "It's been too long since I've done that."

Jeanne smiled.

Nancy continued to search her memory, unwilling to let go of the pictures that obviously played out in her head. "Real trees are messy, having to pick up all the needles that shed. I'll never forget someone suggesting that we get a fake tree. I thought both of my parents were going to have a stroke."

Jeanne laughed.

"My papa would also let me hang our giant green Christmas ball; it was a porcelain heirloom from the old country."

"Old country?"

"France."

"Right," Jeanne said.

"As far back as I can recall," Nancy explained, "every Christmas Eve, my papa would tell me about the story of Jesus' birth in Bethlehem."

She took a deep breath before her eyes glassed over and she returned to a kinder time.

~ ~ ~

"Christmas means the mass of Christ," Papa explained to his daughter, "and it all began with the birth of Baby Jesus in Bethlehem. Saint Luke wrote that Mary, the wife of Joseph from Nazareth, gave birth to their first-born son, wrapped him in swaddling clothing, and then laid him in a manger because there was no room for them at the inn."

"That stinks," young Nancy said.

"And while shepherds kept watch over their flock that night, an angel appeared to them, telling them not to be afraid; that he was there to bring good tidings of great joy—because Christ the Lord had been born."

No matter how many times she'd heard it, Nancy's skin always turned to gooseflesh when hearing the blessed tale. "Wow!" she said.

"Yup, wow is right," Mama called out from the kitchen.

"Tell me the whole story, Papa," Nancy pleaded, "and don't leave anything out."

Papa stopped trimming the tree and took a seat beside his girl. "Long ago," he began, smiling, "even before your mom was born…"

Mama's hearty laugh echoed from the kitchen.

"Two thousand years ago, right, Papa?"

"That's right. When King Herod ruled Judea, God sent the angel Gabriel to a young woman named Mary, who was engaged to marry Joseph from Nazareth. Gabriel told Mary, 'Peace be with you. God has blessed you and is pleased with you.' Mary was obviously shocked by this and didn't understand what the angel meant. 'Don't be frightened,' Gabriel said, 'God has chosen you to become impregnated by the Holy Spirit.

You will give birth to a baby boy and you will name him Jesus.' Although she was scared, Mary loved God and trusted him. 'As God chooses,' she told the angel. Gabriel also told Mary that her cousin, Elizabeth—who was too old to have children—would give birth to a baby boy, chosen to prepare the way for Jesus."

"That must have been a lot for Mary to hear," Nancy said, innocently.

"I'd say," Mama called out from the kitchen, while she continued to bake.

"Joseph must have been very upset that Mary was expecting a baby before they'd been married," Papa continued. "According to the Bible, he considered cancelling the wedding—but that's before an angel also appeared to him in a dream. 'Don't be afraid to take Mary as your wife,' the angel told him, 'Mary has been chosen to give birth to God's Son, who you will name Jesus. The name means...'"

"Savior," Nancy interrupted, "because he was sent to earth to save people."

"Exactly," her papa said, patting her knee. "And Joseph believed the angel's message, so he married Mary."

"Smart man," Mama teased loudly.

Papa chuckled.

"Just before Mary was ready to give birth, the Romans ordered that everyone return to the villages their families came from, so they could collect taxes. Because Joseph's family came from Bethlehem—a long way to walk—he and Mary needed to travel there. When they reached Bethlehem..."

"They had trouble finding a place to stay," Nancy proudly added.

"That's exactly right," her papa said. "Every room was full and there wasn't an empty bed in all of

Bethlehem. The only place they could think to stay was in a barn."

"With the animals," Nancy added.

Papa nodded. "That's right, love. And right where those animals slept, Mary gave birth to Jesus, the Son of God."

"That's so amazing," Nancy whispered.

"Amen to that," Mama echoed from the other room.

Papa said, "They wrapped the newborn in a cloth called swaddling before placing Baby Jesus into the manger where the animals ate their hay."

"Oh, the manger," Mama repeated, causing Nancy and her papa to exchange a knowing glance.

"In the fields outside of Bethlehem," Papa continued, "shepherds looked after their sheep through the long night. As the new day began, an angel appeared before them. Although they must have been very scared, the angel told them, 'Don't be afraid. I have good news. Today, in Bethlehem, a Savior has been born for you. You will find the baby lying in a manger.' Many more angels appeared, singing, 'Glory to God in highest, and peace to his people on earth.' Once the angels had gone, the shepherds went to Bethlehem and found Mary and Joseph. The baby Jesus was lying in a manger, exactly as they'd been told. When they saw him, they told everyone what the angel had said, praising God for sending his Son to be their Savior."

"What about the star?" Nancy asked, impatiently.

"When Jesus was born, a bright star appeared in the sky. Three wise men, who studied the stars and knew a great king had been born, set out to find the baby and bring him gifts."

"Three wise men," Mama called out. "Hmmmm."

Grinning, Papa continued. "The Wise Men followed the star and when they reached Jerusalem, they began to ask, 'Where is the child who is born to be king of the Jews?' Herod, the cruel king of Judea, heard this. It made him very angry that someone might take his place as king, so he sent for the wise men to appear before him. He told them to go on following the star until they'd found the baby king. 'When you've found him,' he'd said, 'let me know where he is, so that I can go and worship him.' But Herod was lying. He was really planning to kill the new king."

"Oh, no," Nancy said.

"The wise men followed the star toward Bethlehem, where it shone directly down on Jesus," Papa said. "Bowing before the baby, the wise men offered their gifts of gold, frankincense and myrrh. But they did not report back to Herod. Instead, they returned to their homes in the East."

"Thank God," Nancy said.

"Thank God, indeed, baby girl," Papa whispered.

~ ~ ~

Returning to the present, Nancy began to cry.

"Please don't be sad, Mrs. Guillmette," Jeanne said.

"Oh, I'm not sad, dear. I'd just..." She stopped to collect herself. "I'd just forgotten how much I was loved." She wiped her eyes. "There are some wonderful people waiting for me up there." She gestured toward the ceiling.

"I'm sure there are," Jeanne said, "but do you think they could share you with me for a little while longer?"

Wearing the biggest smile, the senior nodded. "For a little while," she whispered.

"Perfect," Jeanne said.

"Once Papa finished his story about Baby Jesus," Nancy continued, "Mama would bring a candle-lit cupcake into the living room and we'd sing 'Happy Birthday' to Jesus at the top of our lungs."

"That's wonderful," Jeanne said.

"And then I'd blow out the candle for Jesus."

"What a beautiful tradition," Jeanne said.

"It really was," Nancy agreed. "It was the perfect reminder of the reason for the season." She shook her head, disgustedly. "I passed the tradition on to my girls, but they never stuck with it."

"Oh, no," Jeanne blurted, before scrambling to change the subject. "Why don't you get some rest and eat a few bites, then we can pick it up again tomorrow."

"No," Nancy said, "how 'bout we pick it up a little later—after lunch?"

"Are you sure?" Jeanne asked. "I don't want you to . ."

"I'm sure. I don't want to wait any longer to share these Christmas stories." She paused in thought. "My Christmas story."

Jeanne nodded. "I understand," she said. "You're doing some great work, you know."

"No," Nancy countered, grabbing her new friend's hand, "you're the one who's doing great work."

~ ~ ~

With a wrinkled brow, Jeanne grabbed the telephone receiver. *I never get calls at work,* she thought, *I hope something's not wrong with Lexi.*

"Hello?"

"Hi, Ms. Dube, it's Lorna...Mrs. Guillmette's daughter."

"Oh, hi Lorna," she said, feeling relieved, "and please call me Jeanne. What can I do for you?"

"I was hoping to get an update on my mom. You said that you were going to work with her on some long-term..."

"She's doing just great," Jeanne interrupted. "It's amazing how far back she can go."

"Really?" Lorna said, the surprise in her voice apparent.

"All the way back to her childhood when she was a little girl," Jeanne reported.

Lorna sighed. "That makes me happier than I can tell you, Jeanne. Thank you."

"It's been my pleasure, Lorna—honestly."

"My family's leaving the day after Christmas," the woman said, "and I plan to come in to spend some time with her."

"That's great," Jeanne said, "I'm sure your mom will be very happy to..."

"Can you please not tell her, though?" Lorna asked. "I'd like it to be a surprise."

"Of course," Jeanne said, thinking, *I doubt I'll ever see this woman again.*

There was an awkward pause. "You're probably thinking that I'm just selling you a bill of goods," Lorna said, "but I'll definitely be in to visit with her."

Good, Jeanne thought.

"Teresa and my mom have always been like oil and water," Lorna explained, as though sitting in confession. "And I'm not proud of it, but I've drifted away from her in recent years and..." She paused, collecting herself. "...and I need to change that."

"Good," Jeanne repeated, surprised that the word had escaped her lips this time. "But you don't need to explain any of this to me. I'm just..."

"I know that," Lorna interrupted, "but I love my mother and I'm so grateful for what you're doing for her."

"Like I said, it's been my pleasure," Jeanne told her.

"Thank you," Lorna said, sighing in relief. "Merry Christmas."

"Thanks, but it's already been the merriest Christmas I've had in years," Jeanne said, "I hope you and your family enjoy the same. We'll see you in a few days."

"I'll be there," Lorna confirmed.

"I can't wait for you to see the progress your mom's already made," Jeanne added.

"I look forward to it. Goodbye."

"Goodbye," Jeanne said, hanging up with a smile on her face.

~ ~ ~

"Are you ready to begin again?" Mrs. Guillmette asked, grinning.

"Only if you ate lunch," Jeanne said. "Did you?"

"Of course I ate lunch," the woman said. "These walks down memory lane are exhausting and I need all the energy I can get."

"Exactly!" Jeanne said, nearly squealing with joy. Without thinking, she bent over and gave her patient a long hug—surprised at how strongly Mrs. Guillmette squeezed her back. "I'm all ears when you're ready, Mrs. Guillmette."

Nancy nodded. "My papa said that the Nativity scene originated in Italy, where they still celebrate it today. Evidently, they believe that La Befana—a fairy queen or witch—leaves gifts for children. According to the legend, the three wise men stopped during their journey and asked an old woman for food and shelter. She refused them and they continued on their way. When she had a change of heart, the Magi were long gone—and she's still trying to make up for it."

"Oh wow," Jeanne said, pleased that the storyteller's eyes were still locked on her and not staring off into the past.

"My family couldn't afford a nativity, which I know Mama always wanted. 'Someday,' she'd say, repeating those same words every year." Although Nancy shook her head, her bright eyes were still in the moment. "It really bothered me that Mama didn't have a nativity. If anyone deserved one, it was her. I also remember that I was just as troubled that I never had a birthday present to give to Jesus. And that's when I had my big idea!" She smiled, proudly.

"What big idea?" Jeanne asked, sliding to the edge of her seat.

"Like I said, I felt really bad that Baby Jesus didn't have a place to stay." she said. "That the poor child had to sleep in a manger with the all of the animals. So, without telling anyone—I took a roll of tin foil and formed it into a bed. Then I took one of my dolly's blankets and placed it into the middle of that homemade bed. When I was done, I slid it under the Christmas tree and left it there."

"Oh my God," Jeanne muttered, overcome with a wave of raw, unexpected emotion.

"A few days later, Papa spotted it and asked me what it was," Mrs. Guillmette explained. "I told him, 'It's a bed for Baby Jesus, so that he'll have a place to sleep. Can we please keep it under the tree?' Papa hugged me. 'Of course we can,' he said. 'I don't think there's anything more important than letting Jesus know that He's welcome in our home.'"

"Oh, Mrs. Guillmette," Jeanne said, tears streaking down her cheeks.

The old woman nodded. "I made that same bed every Christmas from then on. It became another of our family's annual Christmas traditions."

"Amazing..."

"That Christmas morning, my stocking was filled with a sweet orange and figs, rock candy and peppermint sticks. And, as always, there was a wooden trinket carved by my papa's own hand."

"Wonderful," Jeanne said, at a loss for more words.

"I unwrapped my one Christmas present under the tree," Nancy said. "It was a baby doll, and I named her Susan, as though I was naming a real child." She wiped a long-forgotten tear from her eye. "Mama had made me a rag doll, wrapped in a dress that had the same exact pattern as my Sunday dress." She chuckled. "I told Mama how strange I thought that was. But she only smiled." The old sage looked up and locked eyes with Jeanne. "It was the type of smile that hinted she knew something but wasn't letting on."

Jeanne nodded.

For a moment, Nancy's eyes drifted off. "We had so little," she said, sighing heavily, "but we had everything."

"You sure did," Jeanne agreed.

"I've forgotten how much I miss my parents. They were such wonderful people and I was so blessed to be raised by them."

Jeanne nodded again. "Tin foil?" she questioned. "I've never heard of that. You mean aluminum foil, right?"

"We called it tin back in my day," Nancy said, smiling. "And I don't care what they make it with now, it'll always be tin foil to me."

"Fair enough," Jeanne said. "The tin foil manger, it is."

Chapter 6

Christmas Eve finally arrived. Nancy sat in front of the dayroom window, staring into the gray sky. "I hope it snows tonight," she said.

"It sure would make it a lot easier for Santa and his reindeer," Jeanne said as she approached.

Nancy smiled, looking up.

"Mrs. Guillmette, I'd like you to meet my daughter, Alexis."

The thirteen-year old girl stepped forward and extended her hand. "My friends call me Lexi," she said, "and it's a pleasure to finally meet you, Mrs. Guillmette. My mom won't stop talking about you."

Jeanne blushed.

"All good, I hope?" the old woman teased.

"Are you kidding," Lexi said, "she absolutely loves you."

Jeanne's pink cheeks turned red. "Lexi, I don't think..."

"Well, that's a mutual feeling, dear," Nancy said, "I absolutely love your mother, too. In fact, I'm pretty sure she's saved my life." She looked at her compassionate nurse and winked. "Or the best part of my soul, anyway."

Jeanne's eyes filled. "Mrs. Guillmette loves holiday traditions," she told her daughter before breaking down and crying. "You can't believe how much she knows about the different ways people celebrate all over the world."

"That's great," Lexi said, smiling at the gentle woman in the wheelchair.

"Do you have any holiday traditions that you enjoy with your family?" Nancy asked the grinning teen.

Lexi nodded. "Since I can remember, we've visited the LaSallette Shrine in Attleboro to see all the lights," she said.

"How many lights are there?" Mrs. Guillmette asked.

"Like the stars in the sky," Lexi said. "I love going there, but it seems that we always go on the coldest night of the year..."

"...with the wind stinging our faces and all the feeling in our hands completely lost," Jeanne added, laughing. "Then we stand in line for an hour to pay good money for hot chocolate that tastes like boiled water."

Nancy joined her in the laughter.

"But it doesn't matter," Lexi said, "as long as we can check those lights off the list every year."

Jeanne placed her arm around her daughter's shoulder, giving it a squeeze.

"We also go to that place where the trains are," Lexi said, struggling to remember the name.

"It's called Edaville Railroad," Jeanne said.

"That's right," Lexi said, excitedly, "and they sell the best mini donuts I've ever eaten." Her eyes went wide. "They're covered in sugar and cinnamon."

"Sure, but we don't go there for the mini donuts," Jeanne told Nancy. "We go to see the lights and ride the train."

"Those donuts sound good, though," Nancy said.

Everyone laughed.

Jeanne looked at her daughter. "Lexi, why don't you tell Mrs. Guillmette what our two newest Christmas traditions are."

"Well, the other night, my mom and I…"

"Mrs. Guillmette," Jeanne blurted, interrupting Lexi, "would you mind if Lexi and I carried on your tradition of the tin foil manger?"

Nancy gasped. "Oh, that would be…" She stopped, allowing her tears their due. "That would be lovely, sweetheart. I'd be honored." Once she gathered herself, she whispered, "I'd always hoped my grandkids would…" She stopped again. "But…" She began to weep.

"We have a few surprises for you tonight," Jeanne said, trying to move beyond the melancholy. "That's if you don't mind?"

While her sobs turned to sniffles, Nancy nodded her approval.

Grabbing the handles on the wheelchair, Jeanne pushed Nancy toward the Christmas tree. "Go ahead and show her," she instructed her daughter.

Dropping to her knees, Lexi crawled under the tree. A moment later, she squirmed back out, dragging a tin foil manger. "And this one's yours, Mrs. Guillmette," the girl announced.

Nancy gasped again. "Oh sweetheart, you have no idea what this means to me."

As if on cue, two male orderlies approached the group. Grabbing the tree, they slowly turned it onto its side, so that the top was only inches from Nancy's reach.

The old woman looked up, confused.

Jeanne handed her a silver star. "We thought it was only right that you did the honors."

Nancy nodded and, with trembling hands, added the final touch to the tree.

As the men pulled the tree upright, Lexi approached the shocked elder—holding a candle-lit cupcake. Through all of the tears, everyone sang, "Happy Birthday" to Jesus.

Once Lexi lowered the cupcake, it took three tries before Nancy blew out the candle for her Savior. "Happy birthday, Lord," she whispered. Then, through her healing tears, she looked up at Lexi.

"Mom says this is also a new tradition we're going to do every year from now on." She smiled. "I hope that's okay with you, Mrs. Guillmette?"

Unable to speak, Nancy grabbed the girl's hand and brought it to her lips where she planted a long kiss.

Nancy then looked up at Jeanne and, when her crying allowed it, she said, "Jeanne, I feel like my mama and papa are right here with me tonight."

Jeanne nodded. "I'm sure they are," she whispered.

"These are the greatest Christmas gifts I've ever received," she said. "How can I ever thank you?"

"You already have, Mrs. Guillmette."

"But...but I didn't give you anything..." Nancy stammered.

Jeanne laughed until her tears would not allow it. "Mrs. Guillmette, you gave me everything." She nodded. "You gave me Christmas."

Lexi hugged her mom.

Jeanne wiped her eyes. "Now is there any chance I can get you to eat something, Mrs. Guillmette?" she asked.

"It depends on what it is," the sobbing woman teased.

"Well, it's your recipe, so I'm guessing it'll be good."

"You made my mama's gorton?" Nancy asked, excitedly.

"She sure did," Lexi said, "and she was careful not to use too much cinnamon."

"Wonderful," Nancy said. "Just wonderful. Let's eat then. I'm starving."

~ ~ ~

A few hours passed before everyone went home for the night. *What a magical Christmas,* Nancy thought, yawning, *but I'm so tired...* She closed her eyes.

~ ~ ~

Little Nancy sat in her papa's lap. "I'm getting tired," she yawned. "When is Santa Claus going to be here?"

"Soon, sweetheart," Mama said, looking up from her mending.

"That's right, but he has lots of kids to visit tonight," Papa added.

"Kids just like me?" Nancy asked.

"Just like you, yes," Papa said, "although their beliefs may be very different from yours."

"Remember, Nancy," Mama said, "people might do things differently from the way we do them, but that doesn't make it wrong."

"Just different," Nancy blurted.

"Exactly!" Papa said. "It's important that we respect the ways of others, as we expect them to respect our traditions. And when you meet someone who is different, there's so much you can learn from each other—because we are all different." Looking out the window, he shook his head. "Santa's gotta be close by now..."

"But I'm pretty sure he doesn't deliver presents to kids who are still awake," Mama added.

Nancy jumped down from her papa's lap. Giving each of her parents a kiss, she hurried off to her bedroom. "I'll go straight to sleep," she promised over her shoulder.

"Good thinking," Papa called back. "Sweet dreams, baby girl."

About the Author

Steven Manchester is the author of the #1 bestsellers *Twelve Months*, *The Rockin' Chair*, *Pressed Pennies*, and *Gooseberry Island* as well as the novels *Goodnight, Brian* and the national bestsellers *The Changing Season* and *Ashes*. His work has appeared on NBC's *Today Show*, CBS's *The Early Show*, CNN's *American Morning*, and BET's *Nightly News*. Recently, three of Manchester's short stories were selected "101 Best" for the *Chicken Soup for the Soul* series.